SHRINK RAP

Robert B. Parker

LARGE PRINT

Oxford

Copyright © Robert B. Parker, 2002

First published in Great Britain 2002
by John Murray (Publishers) Ltd.

Published in Large Print 2003 by ISIS Publishing Ltd,
7 Centremead, Osney Mead, Oxford OX2 0ES
by arrangement with John Murray (Publishers) Ltd.

British Library Cataloguing in Publication Data
Parker, Robert B. (Robert Brown), 1932–
  Shrink rap. – Large print ed.
  1. Randall, Sunny (Fictitious character) – Fiction
  2. Women private investigators – Massachusetts
  – Boston – Fiction
  3. Detective and mystery stories
  4. Large type books
  I. Title
  813.5'4 [F]

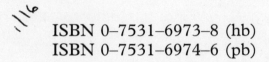

        ISBN 0–7531–6973–8 (hb)
        ISBN 0–7531–6974–6 (pb)

Printed and bound by Antony Rowe, Chippenham

Joan, Dave, Dan . . .
I'll tell them I remember you.

CHAPTER
ONE

I always loved Richie's hands. They looked like such man's hands. I knew that I was guilty of gross gender stereotyping, but I kept my mouth shut about it, and no one knew. His hands rested on the table between us, the right one on top of the left. They were still. Richie was always still. It was one of the things that had made it hard to be married to him. I knew intellectually that he loved me, but he was so contained and interior that I used to crave even the most unseemly display of feeling. He was still now, sitting across the table from me, telling me he'd met someone else. We were divorced. It was fine for him to see other people. I saw other people too. But this was a somebody else he'd met. This was more than seeing other people. This made me feel like my center had collapsed.

"Somebody, like walk into the sunset?" I said.

"She wants to get married," Richie said. "She has a right to that."

"And you?"

Richie shrugged. "I'm thinking about it."

"Three kids and a house in the western suburbs?"

"We haven't talked about that," Richie said.

"What about Rosie?" I said.

"She likes dogs."

I looked at the hamburger I had ordered. I didn't want it.

"Rosie would still want to visit," I said.

"I love Rosie," Richie said.

"Has Ms. Right met her?" I said.

"Yes."

"They get along?"

"Very well," Richie said. "Rosie loves her."

She does not.

"Rosie will remain my dog," I said.

Richie smiled at me. "We're not going to have a custody fight over a goddamn bull terrier, are we?"

"Not as long as we remember she's mine."

"She's ours," Richie said.

"But not hers."

"No. Mine and yours," Richie said. "She lives with you and visits me."

I nodded. Richie was quiet.

"How long have you been seeing Ms. Right?" I said.

"About three months."

"Three months."

Richie nodded.

"You're sleeping with her," I said.

"Of course."

"Do you love Ms. Right?" I said.

"Her name is Carrie."

"Do you love Carrie?"

"I don't know."

"And how are you going to find out?" I said.

"I don't know."

Richie had ordered a club sandwich, on whole wheat, toasted. He hadn't eaten any of it. The waitress stopped at our table.

"Is everything all right?" she said.

"Fine," Richie said.

"Can I get you anything else?"

"No," Richie said. "Check will be fine."

"Do you want me to have your food wrapped?" the waitress said.

"No thank you," Richie said.

The waitress looked at me. I shook my head. She put a check on the table and went away looking regretful. Richie and I looked at each other.

"Whaddya think?" he said.

I shook my head.

"I know," Richie said.

He looked at the check and took some bills out of his wallet and put them on the table.

"The thing is," he said, "I can't get past you."

"Oh?"

"I mean, we're sort of spinning our wheels."

"You could call it that," I said.

"I mean this is a nice woman, and she's happy with who and what I am."

I nodded.

"But I can't get past you," Richie said.

"I face somewhat the same problem," I said.

"We need some kind of resolution, Sunny."

"I thought the divorce was supposed to be some kind of resolution," I said.

Richie smiled quietly. "I did too," he said.

"But it wasn't," I said.

"No. It wasn't."

"So what are we supposed to do?" I said.

"I'm serious about this woman."

I nodded. It was difficult for me to speak. The room around me seemed insubstantial, as if I were drifting in space.

"But," he said, "I can't imagine a life without you in it."

"So," I said. "What the hell is this, a warning that you're going to try?"

"I guess it is," Richie said.

The room was nearly empty. There was only one other table occupied, by three people calmly having lunch. The waitress stayed away from us. Discreet. I looked at the money that Richie had stacked neatly on top of the bill.

"I miss Rosie," Richie said.

"She misses you."

I was quiet. Richie was perfectly still, his hands folded motionless on the table. We were so silent that I was aware of his breathing across the table.

"Are we really talking about the dog here?" Richie said.

"No," I said, "we goddamned sure are not."

CHAPTER
TWO

Melanie Joan Hall, wearing a considerable hat, sat across from me having breakfast in the dining room of the Four Seasons Hotel. Beside her was the Vice President, Publicity, for Scepter Books, which, very successfully, published Melanie Joan. Beside me was Upton Lake, the publisher's Corporate Counsel.

"If I may cut to the chase," Lake said, "we are asking Ms. Hall to tour on behalf of her new book."

I nodded.

"She was originally scheduled for fifteen cities, but because of the tragic events in New York and Washington . . ."

"And Pennsylvania," I said.

"And Pennsylvania. We are now asking her only to go to cities where she can drive."

"Prudent," I said.

"And we need a competent escort to drive her."

"Admittedly, I'm a swell driver," I said, "but why me?"

"My ex-husband won't leave me alone," Melanie Joan said.

Too bad I can't say the same.

"Melanie Joan has requested security," the Vice President, Publicity, said.

The two women were entirely unalike. Melanie Joan was zaftig and blond in a tight flowery dress with a skirt to mid thigh. The Vice President, Allison Birmingham, was a tall, thin woman wearing a black suit and eyeglasses with green rims. Lake was sporting the full-dress New York corporate look: crisp white hair, ruddy complexion, navy blue suit, red tie, blue striped shirt with a white collar. There was not a question in my mind that if he removed his suit coat he would be wearing wide red suspenders.

"Are you familiar with Melanie Joan's books?" Allison said.

I nodded. I had read one on an airplane once and been unable to finish it, but there seemed no need to share that.

"Her new book is just out," Allison said. "It is going to be her biggest book yet. We're printing seven hundred and fifty thousand copies. And we are asking her to go on a ten-city promotional tour on behalf of the book."

"Not as many perhaps as, say, Steve King, but a substantial number."

Steve.

"So Melanie Joan is in the big leagues."

Allison said, "Absolutely."

Melanie Joan smiled modestly. She was having a toasted bagel. So was Allison. So was I. It wasn't just weight watching. I knew that all three of us had ordered something that could be eaten neatly. Upton was

6

having bacon and eggs and home fries and buttered toast. *Men!*

"Is your ex-husband dangerous?" I said.

"I don't think we know that," Melanie Joan said. "He is very certainly annoying."

"I can probably help with the danger part," I said. "I don't know what I can do about making him less annoying."

"And you're prepared to drive city to city with Ms. Hall?" Upton said.

"That would have something to do with how much you are prepared to pay me," I said.

"We will pay you your usual rate, plus expenses," Upton said. "Ms. Hall, of course, travels first class. So you would as well."

"Where would we go?" I said.

Melanie Joan rattled off the cities in an almost expressionless tone: "Pittsburgh, Cleveland, Cincinnati, Dayton, Louisville, New York, Philadelphia, Baltimore, Washington, D.C."

"Good heavens," I said.

"The tour should take two weeks," Allison said. "It is scheduled to end October thirtieth."

"Four cities a week."

"Yes."

"And you think your ex-husband will be able to keep up the pace?"

"I don't know that he won't," Melanie Joan said.

"You're all from New York, why come up here and offer me the job," I said.

"Melanie Joan still lives here," Allison said.

"And, I might need you beyond the book tour," Melanie Joan said. "If we get along all right."

"A test run," I said. "At the publisher's expense."

Melanie Joan smiled.

"Maybe," she said.

The girls were talking too much, Lake needed to reassert himself. "I called your police commissioner," he said.

"Oh," I said.

"Oh?" Melanie Joan said.

"Pat Reagan used to be my father's partner."

"Your father was a policeman?" Melanie Joan said.

"Yes. He retired as a Captain."

"We checked you thoroughly," Upton said. "Nepotism aside, we're prepared to offer you the job."

"You'd be gone at least two weeks," Allison said.

"Do you have children?" Melanie Joan said.

"No," I said. "I have a dog."

"Will that be a problem?"

"I'll miss her," I said. "But she can stay with her father."

"Your husband?"

"No."

I must have said no with more attitude than I intended. Everyone was silent for a moment.

"So can we count on you?" Allison said.

"Certainly," I said.

CHAPTER
THREE

The sonovabitch," I said to Spike, "has someone else."

"He's thinking of having someone else," Spike said and gave Rosie a french fry under the table. She ate it at once and turned her laserlike gaze back upward at Spike. Rosie was an English bull terrier, a miniature, and when she sat like that she looked a bit like a small black-and-white pyramid, albeit a beautiful one.

"It's not right," I said. "And don't give her french fries."

"Aren't you and Richie divorced?" Spike said.

He gave Rosie another fry.

"Yes, but we had an arrangement."

"Un huh."

"Well, goddamnit, we did."

"Is it anything like the arrangement you had with Brian Kelly?"

Rosie elevated without visible volition onto Spike's lap and lapped his ear.

"That was different," I said.

Spike smiled. He got another french fry off his plate and handed it to Rosie.

"Well, it was," I said. "I wasn't planning to walk off into the sunset with him."

"You never thought about it for a moment?" Spike said.

"Well, of course, sure, naturally you think about it."

Spike was big and powerful in a bearish sort of way. He wasn't bald yet, but his hair had begun to recede visibly. If she couldn't be with me, or Richie, Rosie wanted to be with Spike. She was busy again, lapping. Spike turned his head, to avoid death by saliva. He smiled at me again and didn't say anything. We were in his restaurant; not his actually, but the one that he had free reign to manage. I had a salad, which I wasn't eating. Spike had a lovely cheeseburger and fries, which he was sharing with Rosie.

"Oh, all right," I said.

"Oh, all right?"

"All right, he's not doing anything that I didn't do."

Spike nodded.

"But at least I didn't tell him about it."

Spike nodded again, and smiled again. I wanted to strangle him. Rosie had both forepaws on the table now, her black oval eyes fixed upon the remaining french fries.

"So I'm mad," I said, "because Richie didn't mislead me the way I did him."

"You think?" Spike said.

"Oh, fuck you," I said.

"Good point," Spike said.

"But, my God, Spike, what if he does marry the damned hussy?"

"You want to be married to him again?"

I was quiet for a long time. Spike had a large bite of cheeseburger.

Finally, I said, "I don't know."

"Does he want to be married to you again?" Spike said.

"I don't know."

A man and woman came to the table. Mr. and Mrs. Business: dark suits, briefcases, smooth hair, round glasses. The man's smooth hair was gray. The woman's smooth hair was blond, and other than that, allowing for anatomy, they looked interchangeable.

"Are you the manager?" the man said to Spike.

"Sometimes," Spike said. "But not right now. Right now I'm doing psychotherapy."

The man looked puzzled.

"We're having a problem with our waitress," the woman said.

"Leave her a big tip," Spike said, "and call me in the morning."

"That's your response?" the man said.

"It is," Spike said. He held another french fry for Rosie.

"That's disgusting," the woman said, "feeding a dog from the table in a restaurant."

"She's not having trouble with her waitress," Spike said.

"I'll tell you one thing right now," the man said. "We'll never be back here."

"Promises, promises," Spike said. He smiled at both of them. But there was something in the smile. The man almost flinched. The woman took his arm.

"Come on, Brett," she said. "Let's not get down to his level."

Spike took Rosie off his lap and stood, and sat her on his chair. When he straightened he was still smiling his smile. He pointed at them and then at the door.

"Beat it," he said.

The man started to speak, stopped. The woman pulled on the man's arm until he turned and stalked out with her. Spike picked Rosie back up and sat down and put her back in his lap.

"I guess the customer isn't always right," I said.

"I hate it," Spike said, "when I'm doing therapy, and somebody bothers me."

"I wouldn't have guessed that," I said.

Spike grinned. His eyes were pale blue. They looked amused. They always looked amused. Almost.

"You gonna leave Rosie with him when you go off with this author?" Spike said.

"Yes."

"Even if his girlfriend might pat her?"

"I hate that," I said. "But . . . yes."

We were quiet while Spike finished the cheeseburger. The fries were gone too. He pushed the empty plate close to Rosie so she could lap it.

"Here's what I think," Spike said. "I think Richie won't commit to this broad any more than you would commit to Brian Kelly."

"And that would be, why?" I said.

"That would be because you are both connected to each other in ways you don't even understand yet."

"And you think we will?"

"You'd better," Spike said.

CHAPTER
FOUR

We were on the Mass Pike passing through Lenox, with me driving, heading west with the cruise control set at seventy, two good looking babes in a rental Mercedes, talking.

"Sometimes I think it's so inconsequential," Melanie Joan said, "in the face of the terrorist horror: my books, my silly marriage problems, all of it."

"It is probably consequential to you," I said.

"But what does it matter compared to the awfulness of September eleventh?"

"I don't imagine anything much matters compared to eternity," I said. "It's probably best to keep on doing what you know how to do."

"But doesn't it make you feel vulnerable?" Melanie Joan said.

"Sure," I said. "And angry, and vengeful and scared, and appalled."

"And what do you do with all those feelings?"

"I experience them."

"And move on?" Melanie Joan said.

"Yes."

We stopped at the West Stockbridge tollbooth. I paid and tucked the receipt over the visor. We were in New York State now.

"When we first met," Melanie Joan said, "someone asked about your husband and you were very brusque."

"True."

"Are you having trouble with your marriage."

"I'm divorced," I said.

"Do you feel like talking about it?" Melanie Joan said.

"You first."

Melanie Joan was staring out the window at the rural New York landscape. Up a low hill a large billboard announced the prospect of a motel with a pool and an entertainment center only fifty miles hence.

"It seemed so simple a thing," she said. "I was smart, I was a cheerleader, I would go to college, meet the right man — in my circles that's why girls went to college — and happy ever aftering."

I smiled encouragingly.

"And I did," Melanie Joan said. "In fact I've met the right man a number of times."

"And married them?"

"Every time," she said. "They're bastards, aren't they?"

"Not always," I said. "Richie's not a bastard . . . I don't think."

"Do you ever see each other?"

"Yes. Once a week, on Wednesday nights, when we can."

"How civilized," Melanie Joan said.

"We share custody of a dog, Rosie."

"Children?" Melanie Joan said.

"No. Just Rosie."

"What kind?"

"A miniature English bull terrier."

"I'm not sure I know what they look like."

"Spuds McKenzie?" I said. "In the beer ads?"

Melanie Joan shook her head.

"Well," I said. "They're unusually beautiful."

"My first husband wasn't so bad," Melanie Joan said. "He was nice, really. He just never got over being a college kid. He was still drinking beer, and playing ball, and chasing girls, you know?"

"You divorced him?"

"Yes. I got tired of feeling like a date for spring weekend."

I nodded. Melanie Joan was a striking woman, despite the big hair and the short skirts. She was older than I was, with good cheekbones and lovely skin. Men looked at her, but, then, men look at everyone.

"Number two was a novelist with very little libido."

"Don't you hate when that happens," I said, just to be saying something. "Have I heard of him?"

"I doubt it. That was another part of our problem."

"You were the more successful writer," I said.

Melanie Joan nodded. "And he saw my success as a sellout," she said.

"Probably needed to," I said.

"Probably."

Melanie Joan looked out the window for a moment.

"Of course in his terms, I probably am a sellout. I write sort of high-end bodice rippers."

"Bodice rippers?" I said.

"Feminine romances," Melanie Joan said.

"Can't they be good?" I said.

"They might be, I don't know. Mine aren't."

"Because?"

"Because I can't make them good. I have a talent for telling a story that several million people will want to read. But I'm not a terribly good writer."

"So," I said, "you're doing the best you can."

"Yes," she said. "I suppose I am."

"Which means you're not selling out. You're working at capacity."

Melanie Joan laughed. "I hadn't thought of it that way," she said. "You're very clever."

"A trained detective," I said.

"It has been some sort of downward spiral," Melanie Joan said. "Each time I married I made a worse choice than I had before."

"Which one is the stalker?" I said.

"Third," she said, and smiled without much amusement. "And last."

"It's too soon to give up," I said.

Melanie Joan shook her head and didn't answer.

"Do you really think you can protect me from him?" she said.

"Sure," I said.

"But you're this slender thing."

"I'm quick," I said.

"How did you get to be a detective?" Melanie Joan said.

"My father was a policeman," I said. "I liked the work. But there was too much structure. So I left and . . . voila."

"It's hard to imagine a beautiful girl like you . . ." Melanie Joan shook her head. Mystified.

"It is," I said. "Isn't it."

CHAPTER
FIVE

"Do you actually think of yourself as Melanie Joan?" I said.

We were sitting at the bar off the lobby in the Stouffer's Tower Plaza on Public Square in Cleveland.

"Melanie Joan is part of the public persona," Melanie Joan said. "Like the big hair and the tight dress."

It was quarter to ten at night. We were drinking cosmopolitans. The bar was quiet. It was nearly full but it opened onto the lobby and the vast high arch of the lobby tended to absorb noise.

"When he watched me get dressed for a signing or something," Melanie Joan said, "my first husband would call it "putting on Melanie Joan Hall." When I'm alone, I suppose, I'm probably still a little girl named Joanie."

I smiled, and sipped my cosmopolitan. I looked at it with the translucence from behind the bar shining through it. Mostly I drink them because they look so pretty.

"So what do you wear when you are just being Joanie?" I said.

"I'm almost never just Joanie anymore. Sometimes, in moments of maturity, I'm Joan. When I'm being Joan for long enough, I dress pretty much like you."

"That well," I said.

"You dress very well, Sunny, as you know. Everything is stylish, everything is well cut, you have a wonderful figure, so everything fits, and you look at ease with your clothes and yourself."

"I don't think so," I said.

"Your ex-husband?" Melanie Joan said.

"Yes, well, not really, I suppose. I suppose really it's me."

"And you don't feel like talking."

"Forgive me," I said. "I don't."

"Of course," Melanie Joan said.

A large sort of clumsy-looking young man came toward us. He had pale skin and small eyes and dark hair that fell fetchingly over his forehead.

"You ladies far from home," he said.

Melanie Joan's face tightened and she seemed to shrink in on herself.

She said, "Sunny."

I was already facing him. I took my purse from the bar and put it in my lap and opened it. Melanie Joan turned slowly toward him.

"I'm from Indianapolis," he said.

I could see Melanie Joan's shoulders relax.

"Hello," she said. "I'm Melanie Joan. This is my friend Sunny."

Back in character.

"What kind of name is Sunny?" he said.

20

"Mellifluous."

He gave me a big smile.

"Hey that's good," he said. "I like confident girls."

"I'll bet," I said.

He looked blank for a moment, then readjusted his smile.

"My name's Marc," he said.

"Hi, Marc," Melanie Joan said.

"Can I buy you ladies a drink?"

Melanie Joan said, "Certainly."

Marc looked at me. I shook my head.

"Hey, aren't you supposed to be sunny?" Marc laughed happily at how clever he was. "Your name's Sunny."

"Sunny is short for Sonya," I said. "I'm being very Sonya."

Marc had no idea what I was talking about, but I could see him decide that he was not going to get me into bed tonight. He turned to Melanie Joan.

"What are you drinking?"

"I'd love another one of these lovely cosmopolitans," she said.

"You got it," Marc said and gestured to the bartender.

"Another one for the lady," he said, "and a Crown and Coke for me."

The bartender looked at me. I shook my head. The bartender went and mixed the drinks and brought them back.

"So what do you do?" Marc said.

"Melanie Joan."

"Melanie Joan," Marc said. "What do you do?"

"Nothing," Melanie Joan said.

Marc frowned, his small eyes squinching up. He took a needful pull on his Crown and Coke.

"Nothing?"

"Nope," Melanie Joan said, "not a thing."

"You married?"

"Not at the moment."

"I'm separated," Marc said.

He drank some more Crown and Coke, his eyes already checking to see if the bartender was standing by. His suit, I noticed, fit him badly.

"Were you married long?" Melanie Joan said.

"I was never married," Marc said. "The old lady was married but not me, you know what I mean."

"No, I don't," Melanie Joan said.

"Well, ah, I mean, I was sort of, ah, footloose, you might say," Marc said.

"I might," Melanie Joan said.

Marc ordered himself another drink. Melanie Joan declined another.

"So," Marc said, "how come your friend's such a sourpuss?"

"Maybe because she thinks you're a boring jerk," Melanie Joan said.

"Hey," Marc said. "That's no way to talk."

"You asked," Melanie Joan said.

"For crissake, I just bought you a drink."

"You did," Melanie Joan said, "didn't you."

She opened her purse and took out a five-dollar bill and handed it to him.

"Beat it," she said.

He held the bill for a moment, then let it drop to the floor.

"Fuck you," he said, and turned and walked back to his table.

"Ah, the single life," I said.

Melanie Joan nodded, watching Marc move clumsily away.

"It seems that you started out being Melanie Joan and switched to Joan in mid sentence."

"He wasn't a fan," she said and smiled at me.

CHAPTER
SIX

Melanie Joan, in full Melanie Joan Hall regalia, was seated at a table in the open space, near the cash registers at the front of the Regal Bookstore in Shaker Heights. A patient line of people, mostly women, ran back among the aisles of the bookstore.

"Hi," Melanie Joan said to the fifty-third woman who stopped at her table. "How are you? It's nice to see you."

"It's for my mother," the woman said.

"And what is her name?" Melanie Joan said. Her smile was wide and welcoming and seemed genuine.

"Gertrude," the woman said.

As she wrote on the title page of the book, which a bookstore associate had opened for her, Melanie Joan talked to the woman.

"Gertrude? I had an aunt named Gertrude, though out here I suppose you say 'ant'."

The woman smiled and looked at her book and said thank you and moved on. I was standing near the door behind Melanie Joan, with my arms folded. Books were signed. Melanie Joan chatted with each person. The chatting made it seem leisurely and personal but Melanie Joan signed very swiftly.

"Could we have our picture taken with you?" a young woman asked Melanie Joan.

"Absolutely. Sunny, you snap the picture."

One of the young women handed me a yellow cardboard disposable camera.

"Just push the flash button and when it's red in the viewer press the other button."

"Got it," I said.

The young women went around the table and stood on either side of Melanie Joan. I went around in front of the table and aimed the camera.

"Here, let me stand up," Melanie Joan said.

She stood and put her arms around the two young women, probably sisters, one on each side of her.

"Girlfriends," she said with a wide smile.

I pressed the flash button. It showed red in the viewfinder. I centered on Melanie Joan. She was looking past me into the middle distance, the way people do who've been photographed a lot. Her eyes suddenly widened and her smile became suddenly fixed. I snapped the picture and turned and looked in back of me down the aisle where she had been looking. Among the women, halfway up the aisle, was a guy who looked like Clark Kent. He was wearing dark-rimmed glasses. His face was pleasingly square. His jaw was strong. His black hair was longish, but expensively barbered. He wore a rust-colored Harris tweed jacket over a black wool turtleneck, tan corduroy trousers, and some sort of rough-finish tan hiking shoes, the kind people who don't hike wear. He was carrying Melanie Joan's latest book and looked very pleased to be him.

I gave the camera back to the young ladies. They thanked me and Melanie Joan and me again and Melanie Joan twice more and moved on. Melanie Joan seemed frozen.

"That him?" I said with my back to Clark Kent. "With the glasses."

Melanie Joan nodded stiffly.

"Sit back down," I said. "And be Melanie Joan some more. I'm right here."

Melanie Joan didn't move.

"Don't let the bastard keep you from doing what you do," I said softly.

The bookstore personnel were glancing at Melanie Joan.

"Sit," I said.

She stepped to her chair and sat and smiled at a red-haired woman with a baby in a belly pack who stood in front of her holding out her book. I went back to my place and looked at Clark. He was oblivious of me. I'm sure he didn't see me. His whole focus was Melanie Joan, and his eyes stayed fixed on her as the line shortened.

"Can you make it out to Alice?" the red-haired woman said. "And date it?"

"Sure," Melanie Joan said.

She pointed to the baby.

"Is this Alice?"

"Yes," the red-haired woman said with a big smile.

Melanie Joan signed *To Alice whom I met early, and hope to meet again, love Melanie Joan Hall.*

26

Melanie Joan handed the signed book back to the red-haired woman and she moved on with her baby. Clark Kent got another place closer.

"I can't," Melanie Joan said to me under her breath.

"Sure you can," I said. "I'm right here."

Melanie Joan signed another book for a small man with his pants belted somewhere up near his chest.

"My wife reads all your books," he said.

Melanie Joan smiled warmly and handed him back his book. The woman in front of Clark Kent was wearing a ghastly pink pants suit. She picked up a book from the pile on the table.

"Do I give you the money?" she said to Melanie Joan.

Melanie Joan smiled and shook her head. The smile was stiffer than it had been. The bookstore assistant manager was supervising operations at the autograph table.

"You pay the cashier up front," the assistant manager said. "Would you like Miss Hall to sign it for you?"

"No thanks," she said and took the book and headed to the front of the store.

I would have wondered what she stood in line for, if I weren't so interested in Clark Kent. He stood in front of Melanie Joan smiling down at her. Behind the big dark-rimmed glasses his eyes had endearing crinkles.

"Could you sign my book for me, Mrs. Melvin?"

I stepped a little closer to Melanie Joan, trying to be reassuring. He never looked at me. Melanie Joan took the book without looking at him and signed it with her

27

practiced scrawl, *Melanie Joan Hall*. He picked the book up and stared at the signature.

"Could you personalize it?" he said.

His gaze was very steady on Melanie Joan. She didn't look up. I stepped in behind him.

"There's a substantial line, sir," I said to him. "I'm sorry, but Ms. Hall will just be doing signatures."

He didn't look at me.

"She has personalized for other people," he said, looking down at Melanie Joan.

His voice was mild. But its lack of affect was chilling.

"I'm sorry," I said. "Signature only."

"And you are?" he said.

"Just a faceless bureaucrat," I said. "In charge of signatures."

He looked at me thoughtfully. The store people knew who I was. They were getting more uneasy.

"I'm sorry, sir, but there are a lot of people waiting," the assistant manager said. "I'll have to ask you to move along."

Clark Kent looked at the assistant manager for a moment without any expression, then he looked at me in the same empty way. It was as if I weren't there. I had no sense that I registered on his screen. Finally he looked down at Melanie Joan.

"Well, Melanie Joan," he said. "Maybe next time."

Melanie Joan, still looking down at the tabletop, shook her head. He smiled at the top of her head and then spoke to me without looking.

"Will I see you again?" he said.

"It is hard to predict where life will lead us," I said.

"Are you escorting Mrs. Melvin?"

"I'm with Miss Hall," I said.

"The former, by several, Miss Hall," he said, looking at Melanie Joan, who looked at the tabletop. "Are you a book tour escort?"

"At the moment," I said.

"So you'll be traveling with Mrs. Melvin throughout her tour?"

I didn't say anything. All this not looking was getting pretty contrived. She doesn't look at him. He doesn't look at me. I wanted to give him a big kick.

"Sir," the assistant manager said, "please."

Clark Kent didn't say anything. He looked straight down at Melanie Joan's lowered head for another moment. Then, carefully ignoring me, he tossed the book on the floor and turned and walked from the store. Nobody said anything. Everyone stared at the book, open facedown on the floor, with one flap of the dust jacket splayed loose.

Melanie Joan's shoulders were shaking, and her hands trembled. I put my hand on her shoulder and turned to the assistant manager.

"Miss Hall will do only signatures from here on," I said.

"Of course," the assistant manager said, and began informing people along the still-substantial line.

CHAPTER
SEVEN

It was raining. Not a steady rain, so I could leave the wipers on and forget it, but bursts of it that lasted for a while and stopped abruptly, and began as suddenly as it had stopped.

"Maybe the rain is constant," I said, "and we're driving in and out of it."

We were on Route 71 driving southwest toward Kentucky. Melanie Joan was looking straight out the front window at the inconstant downpour. She nodded without any sign that she'd actually ingested what I said.

"Maybe," she said.

"Depressed?" I said.

She didn't answer for a moment. We were in mid-rain burst. Then she looked at me and said, "What?"

"Are you depressed about your husband?"

"Depressed? Yes. And frightened."

"Because?"

"Why am I frightened?"

"Mm hm."

She looked at the rain for a moment, flooding down the wind-shield, kept barely at bay by the wipers.

"I don't know," she said. "He's frightening. I guess I think he's so self-absorbed that he is capable of anything that would serve himself."

"Were you afraid of him when you were married?" I said.

"No, yes, no, not at first. At first I saw what you probably saw. Good-looking man. Nice clothes, glasses. Cultured, charming."

"He ever hurt you?" I said.

"He never really did, but long before the divorce I became afraid he was going to."

"Did he threaten you?"

"Not exactly."

"Then what frightened you?"

"I don't know. Maybe it's me."

"No," I said. "It's not you."

"How can you be so sure?" Melanie Joan said.

"He looked at me," I said. "I saw his eyes."

"Yes."

"There's nothing human in there," I said.

It was dark on the highway and there was a strong wind behind the rain.

"No," Melanie Joan said so softly I could barely hear her, "nothing."

The highway ahead of us was black and slick and shiny. Melanie Joan stared at it silently. We were the only car on the road. The wipers struggled rhythmically with the downpour.

"Tell me about him," I said.

"I don't like to talk about him."

"You need to tell me about him," I said. "I need to know what I'm dealing with."

"I suppose I'm ashamed of myself for marrying him. Talking about him embarrasses me. I don't quite know where to start."

"What does he do for work?" I said.

"He's a psychiatrist," Melanie Joan said.

"In Boston."

"Yes."

"Private practice?"

"He's on the faculty at Taft Medical School, and he has a private practice in Chestnut Hill."

Melanie Joan looked ahead at the wet highway and almost smiled.

"His practice is largely women," she said.

"How does that happen?" I said.

"I think he prefers women patients."

"And his shingle says 'girls are us'?"

Melanie Joan still couldn't quite smile.

She said, "No. I think he just accepts more women than men for treatment."

"Is he successful?"

"Do you mean has he a big practice? Yes."

"Is he a good psychiatrist?"

"He understands human behavior," Melanie Joan said.

"Meaning?"

"Meaning he can manipulate people."

"And does?"

"Yes."

"Including you?" I said.

"Especially me," she said.

"How does he manipulate you?"

The rain had stopped and there was a gap in the dark clouds through which sunlight shone. The wind seemed to have died. I could hear the sounds of the tires on the highway now.

"With love," Melanie Joan said.

"Giving and withholding?"

"Yes."

"My mother used to do that," I said. "Still does."

"So did my father."

"Ohhh?" I said.

"Yes," Melanie Joan said, "ohhh."

"I will avoid the obvious," I said.

"Thank you."

I glanced over at her, in the passenger seat, wearing the full Melanie Joan. Her appearance didn't go with the conversation.

"John appears to have no interest," she said, "in a woman he can't manipulate."

"To what purpose?" I said.

"I think the manipulation is its own reward," she said.

"His name is John?" I said.

"John Melvin," Melanie Joan said. Her voice was harsh. "M.D."

The rain started again, coming straight in at us now, blown by the reinvigorated wind, as we drove across the unfamiliar Ohio landscape. I felt a long way from home. I missed Rosie. I thought about her, probably sleeping happily in her little bed behind the bar in the tavern Richie's family owned. That evening he'd take her for a walk and they'd play ball and she'd sleep in bed with him in the room that looked out over the harbor, and filled with light when the sun came up.

CHAPTER
EIGHT

We were in our suite at the hotel in Louisville. The living room door was bolted and chained. Melanie Joan was in her bedroom. I was in mine. I had taken off my face, had a bath, washed my hair and now, lying on the bed in my jammies, with my gun on the bedside table, I called Richie.

"Is this a good time?" I said.

"Sure."

"You're alone?"

"No, Rosie's here," he said.

I could hear the smile in Richie's voice.

"How is my baby?" I said.

"I'm fine," he said.

"You know who I mean."

"Yes," Richie said. "I do. She's asleep on the bed beside me. She's leaning sideways against one of the pillows with her feet in the air and her tongue hanging out one side of her mouth."

"How beautiful does she look?" I said.

"As beautiful as she always looks," Richie said.

"Is she missing her mommy?"

"Probably," Richie said. "But she's perky in spite of it."

"And you're walking her?"

"Yep."

"She go with you during the day?"

"Everywhere," Richie said. "To the bar, calling on customers, everywhere."

"What customers do you call on?" I said.

"Customers," he said.

"In the family business."

"Yes."

"Richie, the family business is crime."

"Not my part of it," Richie said.

"I don't understand how you can separate it so precisely," I said.

"I do."

We were quiet, listening to the non-sound the open phone line made.

"How is your trip?" Richie said after a while.

"Fine," I said.

"Where are you now?"

"Louisville," I said. "Has the future Ms. Burke been around?"

"Carrie," Richie said gently. "Yes. She's been around."

"Is she nice to Rosie?"

"She likes Rosie very much," Richie said.

Again the empty noise of the phone.

"I trust you," I said finally. "I know you would make sure that Rosie was all right."

"Of course," Richie said. "You recall that I love Rosie."

"I recall that you once loved me," I said.

Why the hell did I go there?

"Still do," Richie said.

"And Ms. Right?"

"Carrie," he said. "I think so."

"So you can love two women at the same time?"

"That's how it seems," Richie said.

"So where does that leave us?"

Goddamn it.

"I care about Carrie," Richie said. "And you and I can't seem to live together."

"Yet," I said.

"So far," Richie said.

"So maybe I should just get on with my life," I said.

"I thought that's what we were both doing," Richie said. "I thought that was why we got divorced."

"Is that how you want it?"

"Is what how I want it?"

"You wander off into the sunset with whatshername, and we go our separate ways?"

"You know her name is Carrie."

"Whatever," I said.

We were quiet again. I looked at my gun lying near me on the nightstand. Outside my window the rain still came down, sometimes gently, sometimes hard.

"No," Richie said. "That's not how I want it."

I could feel the air begin to stir again in my chest.

"I guess," I said finally, "that neither of us quite knows how we want it."

"Not quite," Richie said. "Not yet."

CHAPTER
NINE

We were in a bookstore in a mall in suburban Cincinnati. Melanie Joan was facing the front of the store at a lectern set in the center of a large circle of folding chairs filled with fans. She was taking questions.

A slender woman with short black hair, dressed in a pink cashmere sweater set, raised her hand with a question.

"Even though they're a little sex-crazed," she said, "your characters seem so real. Are they based on people you know?"

Melanie Joan smiled. "Honey," Melanie Joan said and let the word languish for a moment, "they're all based on me."

The audience laughed. Already, three cities into my first book tour, I had come to understand that most fans came eager to approve.

A small old woman with big eyes and a small sharp nose in the front row said, "Is that true?"

"I kiss and tell," Melanie Joan said and smiled again. It was an impressive smile, wide and warm and apparently spontaneous. "No, not really. When you begin writing I think you probably do use people you know, and clever things you've heard people say. But

38

you use all that up pretty quickly, and you are forced to start imagining the rest."

"How do you work?" a man asked. "Are you a morning person? Do you use a computer?"

"I use a computer," Melanie Joan said, "And normally I . . ."

I was standing behind the circle of fans. Melanie Joan was looking past me at the front of the store. I turned. John Melvin was outside the big front window of the store, pressed against the glass with his arms outstretched above his head. Slowly he brought them down towards his waist and as he did two bright smears of blood followed them. I looked back at Melanie Joan. Without a sound or a change of expression, she put her hands on the lectern for a moment as if to steady herself. Then her hand dropped from the lectern and she slid loosely to the floor and lay still.

"Cops," I said to the store manager. "Ambulance."

I pushed up to Melanie Joan where she lay, and knelt beside her. Her eyes had rolled back in her head. No convulsions. She hadn't swallowed her tongue. Her breath was shallow and a little fast but regular enough. Her pulse was fast, too. As I took her pulse her eyes rolled back down. She looked at me without focus. Her eyelids fluttered.

"Melanie Joan," I said.

Her eyes moved toward me but still without focus. I took her hand.

"Melanie Joan."

A pretty blond woman knelt beside me.

"I'm a nurse," she said. "Has she ever done this before?"

"Not that I know," I said. "She saw something through the front window that shocked her."

The nurse glanced back at the front window with the two dark smears of blood on it.

"What the hell is that?" she said.

"I think she fainted when she saw it," I said.

The nurse nodded. Melanie Joan's eyes began to focus.

"Can you see my hand?" the nurse said to Melanie Joan.

"Of course I can."

Melanie Joan spoke in the over ordinary way we speak when we're awakened suddenly and don't want to admit we were sleeping.

"How many fingers?"

"Three."

"How do you feel?" the nurse said.

"I'm fine," Melanie Joan said. "I'm perfectly fine."

The audience sat as if painted on the backs of its chairs. They didn't know what else to do. In the distance I heard the first siren.

"Can you sit up?" the nurse said.

Melanie Joan nodded. I put a hand under her back, and the nurse took her hand and we raised her to a sitting position. Her short skirt was up high around her thighs. She pulled it down and smoothed it.

"Would you like to sit in a chair?" I said.

Melanie Joan nodded. I jerked my head at the front row and several people vacated their chairs. We got her

40

to her feet and into one of the empty chairs. The sirens were right on top of us now. Through the blood-smeared front window I saw the flashing lights in the parking lot.

"Where is he?" Melanie Joan said to me.

"He's not here," I said. "I'm sure he's run off."

I wasn't so sure he'd run off. That would depend on how much he was bleeding. If it was really his blood, he might be lying in a pallid heap outside the store. But he wasn't. He had in fact run off.

CHAPTER
TEN

When I got home from Cincinnati and dropped Melanie Joan off at her house, I went to pick up Rosie. Rosie was so glad to see me that she tucked her rear end under and raced around Richie's apartment bouncing off walls, bounding onto and off of couches, pausing sometimes to spin in tight pursuit of her own tail. When that was finally over, I got her to settle in with me on the couch in Richie's living room, where I could rub her belly and slowly drink a martini.

Richie was wearing loafers with no socks, faded blue jeans with no belt, and a black polo shirt with short sleeves. His arms were muscular.

"So was it in fact this guy's blood?" Richie said. "On the window?"

"I don't know if it was Melvin's," I said. "But the Cincinnati crime lab says it's human blood. Type A."

"Is that Melvin's blood type?"

"Melanie Joan doesn't know."

"Well, who else's blood would it be?" Richie said.

"It would be hard to imagine," I said.

"He's a psychiatrist?" Richie said.

"Yes."

"That means he's an M.D."

"Yes."

"So he'd probably be able to come by some human blood."

"Yes," I said. "He'd also probably be able to cut himself superficially so as to provide enough of his own."

"So why would he do that?" Richie said.

"Maybe to get the effect he got."

"Make his ex-wife faint?"

"It's a kind of control," I said.

Richie nodded. "How did he know where to find you?" Richie said. "I mean he found you in Cleveland. He found you in Cincinnati."

"I raised that question," I said. "Melanie Joan's publisher, like most of them, puts her tour schedule on their website."

"Book tour over?"

"No. She's going to do some stuff around here. Then we go to the West Coast."

Rosie had a ratty-looking teddy bear she carried around when she felt like it. She had it now and dropped it in my lap and looked at me with her tail wagging. She wanted me to throw it for her so she could get it and bring it back and I'd hold it and she'd tug one end and growl fearsomely. No matter how long I played that game she would outlast me and eventually I would have to say *no*. Logic suggested that I might just as well say *no* now and spare myself. She was giving me her impenetrable black-eyed stare. I threw the teddy bear. She exploded across the room and grabbed it and brought it back and dropped it in my lap and wagged her tail and looked at me with her impenetrable black-eyed stare.

"You squiring her around while she's here?" Richie said.

"I take her to her book signings and return her. If she wants to go someplace other times, she calls me."

I picked up the teddy bear and Rosie immediately clamped onto the other end. She was very strong for a thirty-pound dog, and very enthusiastic. She yanked and tugged and shook her head and I finally let the teddy bear go. Rosie immediately dropped it into my lap again.

"And you sit around between times and wait for her to call?" Richie said.

"Sounds like my dating patterns," I said. "No. I thought in my spare time I'd look into John Melvin a little."

"Because?"

"Because I want to find some way to get him away from Melanie Joan."

"Anything in mind?"

Rosie was yanking on the teddy bear again, all four feet braced stiffly, head down, neck stretched, growling loudly. I let go, she kept her balance and jumped up and put her forefeet on my thighs and dropped the teddy in my lap again.

"Rosie," I said, "could you for God's sake give it a rest."

Rosie wagged her tail and smiled at me.

"I could ask Felix to speak with him," Richie said.

I was quiet for a moment, trying to stare Rosie down. Then I shook my head.

"I know," I said. "I thought of that."

"But?"

"I can't use your uncle to solve my problems."

"Actually he'd be solving Melanie Joan's problems," Richie said.

"Permanently?"

"I think you'd be able to specify."

"Whether I wanted him killed or only crippled?"

"Might not have to be that drastic," Richie said. "He might scare easily."

"I can't, Richie."

"Want me to talk with him?"

"I thought you weren't part of that," I said.

"I'm not. But I could do you a favor, couldn't I?"

I shook my head.

"How about Spike," Richie said. "He could talk to Melvin for you."

I shook my head again.

"I don't mean to sound like an old joke," I said. "But I need to do this myself."

In annoyance Rosie gave me a small nasty yap, and shook the teddy bear in my lap. I patted her. She turned suddenly with her teddy and went over to Richie and dropped the teddy bear in his lap. Richie took one end and she began to tug happily at her end of it.

"You don't sound like a joke," Richie said. "I understand why you need to do it yourself."

We were quiet for a bit, watching Rosie tug on the teddy bear.

"It was sweet of you to offer to have your uncle beat someone up for me."

"We Burkes are a sweet bunch of guys," Richie said.

"Has Ms. Right met your family?"

"Carrie's met my father," Richie said. "I haven't exposed her to Uncle Felix yet."

"And?"

"And she thinks he's sweet."

"How about him?"

"He thinks she's sweet."

"We're all sweet," I said. "Aren't we? You, me, Ms. Right, your hoodlum family, everybody is so fucking sweet."

Richie didn't say anything. I stood much more suddenly than I had intended to, and hooked Rosie's leash on her collar and headed for the door. Rosie seemed a bit puzzled.

"Thanks for offering to kill Melvin," I said.

"Or injure or intimidate," Richie said.

"Whatever," I said. "Thanks for it."

"You're welcome," Richie said.

I went out and slammed the door.

CHAPTER
ELEVEN

Since her divorce, Julie had moved out of the dump she had rented when she left Michael, and bought a one-bedroom condo on the third floor of a converted house off Prospect Street in Cambridge, where she could walk to her office near Harvard Square and do psychological counseling. I met her for dinner in a new place on Main Street called Cuchi Cuchi.

"How are the children?" I said when we were seated.

Julie shrugged.

"It doesn't make me feel good to admit it," she said. "But they seem better than they were when I lived there."

"Isn't that depressing," I said.

"Yes. Except, well, I'm glad they're doing better, whatever the reason."

"Yes."

The waitress brought us menus and took our drink orders.

"Are you still with that writer person?" Julie said.

"Melanie Joan Hall," I said. "Yes."

"Has there been any trouble?"

"Some," I said and told her about our two encounters with John Melvin.

The waitress brought our drinks. A grapefruit gimlet for me. A blackberry cosmopolitan for Julie. We each took a sip.

"Wow," Julie said. "Is that good or what?"

"Mine is delicious," I said.

"Let me taste," Julie said.

We exchanged sips.

"I think this will require more than one," Julie said.

"Only a fool would deny it," I said. "Have you ever heard of a psychiatrist named John Melvin?"

"Melanie Joan Hall's husband?"

"Yes."

"He's a psychiatrist?"

"Yes."

Julie always dramatized everything. She now made a considerable show of running through her memory banks looking for John Melvin. She wasn't being dishonest. Julie was just demonstrative. Finally she shook her head.

"Is he in practice locally?" she said.

"Chestnut Hill, I believe."

"And he does psychotherapy?"

"Yes."

"No," Julie said. "I can't say I know him. That doesn't mean much. There are many fine therapists I don't know."

"I thought you were the nexus of mental health in the Northeast," I said.

"I'm an M.S.W.," Julie said. "Psychiatrists don't mingle with me."

"Well, they should," I said.

Cuchi Cuchi served a number of small plates, tapas-style. I had an order of skewered shrimp to start with. Julie had a salad of Boston lettuce. She looked good. She'd lost weight since her divorce. She wore her dark hair longer, and had changed her makeup.

"Where would be a good place to look for information?"

"Do you know if he does psychoanalysis?"

"I don't."

"Well, if he does, you might try BPSI."

"Bipsi?" I said.

"Boston Psychoanalytic Society and Institute," Julie said. "They're in Boston. And there's the Mass Psychiatric Society, which is, I think, in Waltham."

"How about the Board of Registration?" I said.

"Sure," Julie said. "West Street. And Mass Mental Health on Staniford Street."

"Okay, enough business," I said. "How's your sex life?"

"I'll tell you, if you'll tell me," Julie said.

"Nothing to tell," I said.

"Oh," Julie said. "You too."

I shrugged.

"The nice ones are gay," Julie said. "The straight ones are married . . . or jerks."

"How's Michael?" I said.

"Happily remarried."

"Well," I said. "That kind of brings closure, doesn't it?"

"Kind of," Julie said.

"Have you met her?"

"No."

"What do the kids have to say about her?"

"They seem to like her."

"Oh my," I said.

"Well, it's in their best interests to like her," Julie said.

"I know, but it denies you the secret guilty pleasure you could feel if they hated her."

"Yes," Julie said. "It certainly does."

We ordered two more drinks.

"She's a stockbroker," Julie said.

I nodded. My shrimp was a little hard to get off the skewer. I debated eating it like a chicken leg.

"Michael knew her from work," Julie said.

I decided to cut a bite off of the skewer in a civilized fashion.

"They were dating a month after I left him," Julie said.

I gave up on the knife and fork and picked up my shrimp skewer and took a bite. Excellent.

"Makes me wonder how well they knew each other while we were still married."

"You don't know that," I said.

"It makes you think, though."

"You ever see Robert anymore?" I said.

Julie looked at me for a moment. "You're reminding me that I was fooling around for some time before I left Michael," Julie said.

I shrugged.

"Okay," Julie said. "I'm reminded."

"*Do* you see Robert?" I said.

"No."

Julie finished her salad and most of her second drink.

"Have you seen Richie lately?" Julie said.

"I saw him last night," I said.

"How's that going."

"He has a girlfriend," I said.

"Sort of like that cop Brian Whatsis that you went out with for a while."

"Brian Kelly," I said.

"Do you see him anymore?"

"No."

We sat and looked at each other and after a moment we both began to laugh.

"Well," Julie said. "Let's just keep on dancing."

"I'll drink to that," I said.

CHAPTER
TWELVE

I sat and talked to a tall lean woman with iron gray hair that looked as if it would rattle when she combed it. According to the name plate on her desk, her name was Elsa Earhardt, M.D., and she was an Executive Director.

"Dr. Melvin is a member of our organization," she said. "I can give you his phone number and address."

"Can you tell me anything about him?" I said.

"I don't know him personally," she said.

Her tone was perfectly neutral and a little bit soothing. Her dress was neat and blue. She wore no jewelry. There were degrees in several branches of learning from several universities, none of which I could actually read from where I was sitting.

"Have there been any incidents in his professional life that you could tell me about?"

"I know of none."

"Would you, had there been some?"

"Probably not. We are not a monitoring organization, and if I had learned of anything, ah, incidental, it would very likely be inappropriate for me to discuss them with you."

"Wow," I said.

She raised her eyebrows. "Wow?"

"Yes," I said. "You just foreclosed any avenue of discussion in one declarative sentence."

She smiled in a friendly and approving way. "Surely not every avenue," she said.

"If I had a complaint about him, where would I take it?"

"The Patient Complaints section of the Medicine Registration Board."

"On West Street?"

"I believe so."

"But you can give me his address," I said.

"Certainly," she said. "The receptionist can help you with that."

"Thanks for everything," I said.

"We are not a patient advocacy organization," Dr. Earhardt said. "Our focus is on the physician."

"Well," I said. "Maybe you'd better focus more closely on Dr. Melvin."

She nodded slightly and tipped her head toward me inviting me to speak more.

"He's been obsessively stalking his ex-wife."

"If that were so," Dr. Earhardt said, "it would remain a question for Patient Complaints."

I took one of my business cards out of my purse and handed it across the desk. She took it and looked at it as if it were interesting.

"Sonya Randall," she said. "Investigations, Personal Security."

"That's me," I said. "If something occurs to you, please don't hesitate to call."

She tucked my card carefully into the brown leather corner of her desk blotter.

"I certainly will keep you in mind, Sonya."

I stood.

"Thanks, Elsa," I said and opened her office door and went out.

CHAPTER
THIRTEEN

I took Melanie Joan to an early evening book signing at the vast Barnes & Noble bookstore in Burlington. It was a scene I'd already gotten used to. A table with books stacked up, and an easel with Melanie Joan's picture on a poster. A line of people, most of whom had one of Melanie Joan's books, a couple of store employees lingering near the table to supervise. As we went in I could see Melanie Joan begin to turn into Melanie Joan. She seemed to straighten a little. Her eyes brightened. Without changing expression she seemed more ready to smile. Her step was quicker. I could almost hear theme music begin.

The event coordinator was a young black woman in high-waisted gray pants. Melanie Joan introduced me as her escort. The event coordinator smiled once and ignored me thereafter. Would Melanie Joan like to freshen up? Did Melanie Joan need anything? Water? Coffee? Soft drink? Would she take questions? Did she prefer the microphone fixed on the lectern, or hand-held? Did she have a preference in pens? Felt-tip? Ballpoint? Would she personalize? Would she sign paperbacks? What page did she like to sign on? Melanie Joan knew the answers to all those questions, and threw in two small jokes. I had heard the same two small jokes in Cleveland and Cincinnati and Louisville and Dayton, but each time Melanie Joan said them, they seemed as fresh as if they'd never been said before.

There was a definite murmur in the line when Melanie Joan walked past it to the desk. Several people applauded. Melanie Joan smiled at them brightly. She was wearing black boots with high thick heels, a short gray skirt with a tiny black pattern, and a tight-fitting black top under a silvery leather jacket. She looked like ten million dollars, which, after all, she was.

The bookstore helpers looked at me as if I were going to help with the signing, but I moved away and stood against a shelf of nonfiction titles behind Melanie Joan and a little to the left.

"I'll need an opener," Melanie Joan said to one of the helpers. Then she smiled at the first person in line and put out her hand for a book and said, "Let us begin."

We were on the second floor away from the escalators in a space that had probably been cleared for the event. I looked along the line of fans. John Melvin wasn't among them. I looked past the line at the people who were lingering near the elevator, or walking purposefully toward another section of the bookstore where they could get a book on Tuscan cooking, or personal fitness, or how to reenergize their relationships.

John Melvin was there, leaning his hips against the escalator barrier, his arms folded across his chest. Tonight he was wearing pressed jeans and a black leather jacket with the collar turned up. The collar of his black polo shirt was turned up too, inside the jacket collar. He wore black moccasin-style loafers, and no socks. I looked at Melanie Joan. She gave no sign that she'd seen him.

I had my gun on my belt tonight under my light fall raincoat. It was more a wardrobe decision than a security one. If it didn't ruin my outfit I carried the gun on my belt. If it did, I carried it in my purse. I was conscious of the pleasant weight of the weapon as I walked toward Melvin.

He was looking at Melanie Joan. I could see the hint of bandages on his wrists below the cuff of his jacket. He paid no attention to me. I leaned my hips against the escalator wall beside him and folded my arms like his and said, "How ya doing?"

He turned his head slowly toward me and looked at me with his eyes out of focus and dreamy.

"Excuse me?" he said.

"How ya doing," I said again.

His eyes focused. "Oh," he said. "The faceless bureaucrat. Hello."

"How's the wrists?" I said.

He smiled bravely. "Nothing, really. Just superficial."

"Good to know," I said. "How did it happen?"

"Frankly I'd prefer not to discuss it," he said gently.

"Sure," I said. "What is your interest here tonight?"

"Same as everyone else's, I guess."

"Entirely the same?" I said.

"Well." He smiled. "I have done more with Melanie Joan than read her books."

"For example?" I said.

57

"I used to fuck her," Melvin said.

"Isn't that lovely for you," I said.

"She found it lovely for her," he said.

"But no more," I said.

Melvin looked at me carefully, appraising me, the way people did with horses. "Maybe you will find it lovely."

"Oh, you sweet-talking devil," I said.

He didn't enjoy being kidded.

"Perhaps we'll find out someday," he said.

"Perhaps pigs will fly," I said. "And whistle while they do so."

Something, I don't know quite what, call it a shadow, passed behind his eyes for a moment. It was like seeing the quick slide of a snake in a dark corner. Almost without volition I made sure my coat was open.

"And perhaps you will be less frivolous someday," he said.

I was afraid my voice would be hoarse when I spoke. But it wasn't.

"In the meantime," I said, "you need to understand that Melanie Joan Hall is no longer your wife, and no longer wishes to see you."

"She will see me," he said.

"You know you are pathological," I said.

"Such judgments are mine to make," he said. "Not yours."

"You know it," I said. "And I know it, too."

"It is not a subject for debate," he said. "I will see her when I choose to."

"And you'll see me."

He laughed. There was no humor in the laugh, nor pleasure, nor, for that matter, anything much in the way of humanity. He straightened from his leaning position and stood half a foot taller than I was.

"And what will you do?" he said.

"I might shoot you," I said.

He stared at me. "My God," he said. "You aren't just a tour escort, are you. You're a bodyguard."

"I am," I said.

I opened my coat a little and let him see the gun. He stared at it without an affect. Then he laughed the empty laugh again.

"That makes it more exciting," he said, and smiled the empty smile at me and turned and walked away.

CHAPTER
FOURTEEN

Having gotten not much from Elsa Earhardt, M.D., I thought I might try out a little more routine detecting to see if I was still any good at it. I put Rosie in the car with me and drove over to Chestnut Hill and parked outside the big Victorian house where John Melvin, M.D. had his home and office. It was a lovely big house with white siding and green shutters, and lilac bushes in the front. A brick pathway curved around the side of the house. A small neat sign with a discreet arrow told me that the path led to the office.

I got out two of the tools of my business, a notebook and a ball-point pen.

"Let the adventure begin," I said to Rosie.

She stared out her side of the car, alert for covert squirrel activity. A silver gray Infiniti sedan parked in front of the house and a well-dressed woman got out and walked up the brick path. I wrote down the license plate number. A couple of sparrows foraged on Melvin's small green patch of front lawn. A squirrel hustled past the car with an acorn in its mouth and scooted up a tree. Rosie spotted it and hurled herself around the car gargling and snarling until it was high up in the tree and out of sight.

Everything else that happened was less interesting. Forty-five minutes after the Infiniti had arrived, a beige Mercedes sedan pulled up and parked behind the Infiniti, and another well-dressed woman got out and walked up the brick path. Five minutes after that the first well-dressed woman walked down the path and got into her Infiniti and drove off. In fifty minutes the woman with the Mercedes came out and drove away, and in about another minute a red Subaru wagon pulled in and another woman got out and walked up the path. I now had three license-plate numbers in my notebook.

"A pattern is beginning to develop here," I said to Rosie.

Exhausted by the excitement of the previous two hours, Rosie had curled up on the front seat with one paw up over her nose and gone to sleep. While she slept, the pattern held: once an hour a woman in an expensive car wearing good clothes came for therapy. All of them were attractive. All of them, by my estimate, were somewhere between thirty and fifty. It was hard to tell for sure from where I was across the street, but all of them seemed to have dressed and made up carefully. I was pretty sure you could do therapy in sweats if you needed to, but maybe Melvin had his own rules. Dress for success.

By one o'clock I needed a ladies' room and a sandwich, in that order, and I suspected the same was true for Rosie. So I drove back to Fresh Pond Circle and went into Bread and Circus. I used their ladies' room, spruced up my face and hair, and bought a

Mediterranean sandwich and a quart bottle of water. I took Rosie for a walk around the parking lot, gave her some water, and shared my sandwich with her. Then we went back and looked at John Melvin's brick walk some more. By the end of the day I had eight license-plate numbers, including one of a chauffeured limousine whose driver waited in the car while the lady went in for therapy. Rosie had been even more productive, sighting not only three squirrels but two golden retrievers and a Norwich terrier, all of whom she threatened vociferously from the safety of our car. The owner of one of the goldens had given me a control-your-goddamned-dog glare, which I recognized immediately, having received it before. Up yours, I glared.

When it became apparent that no one else was going to show up at Dr. Melvin's office, I stowed my notebook and drove through rush-hour traffic back to South Boston in the lowering evening.

CHAPTER
FIFTEEN

Brian Kelly had a desk near the window in the detectives' squad room, in the new Area D Station, where he could look down onto Harrison Avenue. He was sitting at the desk, with one foot on a pulled-out bottom drawer. He was wearing a charcoal gray polo shirt and jeans. His badge was pinned to his belt next to his gun.

"Hello darlin'," he said.

I sat in the guest chair beside his desk.

"Hello," I said and handed him the list of license numbers I had accumulated from four days of sitting outside the office of John Melvin, M.D. I'd have gathered a full weeks' worth but Melanie Joan had to make two daytime signing appearances on Thursday. At least Melvin hadn't appeared. I assumed he was busy helping attractive women, which to the best of my ability to observe made up his entire client base.

"Could I help you get listings for these numbers from the Registry?" Brian said.

"How kind of you to offer."

"Like you weren't going to ask," Brian said.

"I was going to ask nicely," I said.

"It's always the same," Brian said. "You ball somebody a few times and they're after you for favors ever after."

"Why do you think somebody balled you?" I said.

Brian grinned at me. "I remember why," he said. "I remember a lot."

I might have blushed. If I did, Brian took no notice. He was a slim man, and very neat, with dark hair cut short. His jeans were pressed. His shoes were shined. The polo shirt might have been new. He was also quite strong, as I remembered, in the wiry way some slim guys have.

"So can you do it?" I said. "For the good times?"

"Sure. I'll fax these over. We'll go have lunch, and the names should be here when we get back . . . if we eat slowly."

"And if I can't do lunch?" I said.

Brian smiled again and handed me back the list without comment.

"Lunch it is," I said.

We ate at a coffee shop full of cops a block from Area D Station. I had a grilled cheese sandwich.

"You back with your husband?" Brian said.

"Not really," I said.

I liked the whispery smell of Brian's aftershave. He ate very neatly, with precise little movements. His eyes were big and brown and kind, although I was sure he could do the dead-eyed cop stare as well as anyone.

"But you haven't shaken loose," Brian said.

"Not yet."

"Seeing anybody else?"

64

"No," I said. "Not at the moment."

"Don't want to?"

"No, I'm happy to date. I just haven't met anyone recently."

"See," Brian said. "Should have grabbed me while you could."

I smiled at him.

"Never say never."

Brian smiled back.

"I'm getting married," he said.

Damn.

"There's a lot of that going around," I said. "Tell me about her."

"She's a first-grade teacher," Brian said. "In Duxbury."

I didn't care if she was Catherine the Great. But I smiled and nodded.

"I got fixed up," Brian said. "Not too long after you and I . . ."

"Congratulations," I said.

"Thank you," he said. "She's great."

"I'm happy for you," I said.

Brian nodded. "You were pretty great too, Sunny."

"Thanks."

"I mean it," Brian said. "You were sensational in bed."

I felt a little uncomfortable. It had been right after I had divorced Richie, crazy time, and I had some extreme moments as I relearned the dating game.

"Yes," I said. "We were good at that."

"You were, are, pretty sensational anyway, Sunny. In or out of bed."

I nodded. I didn't want the rest of my sandwich. I felt as if my throat might close, as if I might cry.

"You okay?" Brian said.

I nodded. "I'm swell," I said. "Perfectly swell."

CHAPTER
SIXTEEN

"You always had Brian in the corner of your mind as a sort of backup person," Julie said. "That's why you feel so bad."

"So if it didn't work out with Richie I always had Brian."

"Something like that," Julie said.

We were at Biba, on Boylston Street, at the downstairs bar, drinking piña coladas.

"I hate to think that of myself," I said.

"Sometimes," Julie said, "the things you hate to think are the ones you have to think about."

"That's such a shrinky thing to say."

"I know," Julie said. "But you knew I was a shrink when you agreed to be my friend."

"Actually," I said, "I was your friend before you were a shrink."

"And have decided to forgive me for it."

"Well," I said. "You're only an M.S.W."

"Good point," Julie said.

We each sipped some piña colada.

"It's hard to be alone," Julie said. "And it's hard to think of yourself alone. I'm going through that too. Your sister went through it last year with that dreadful man."

"Her choices haven't improved," I said.

"You didn't want to fall into that trap," Julie said.

"What trap is that?" I said.

"Without a man I'm insufficient," Julie said.

"Like you did with whatsisname," I said.

"Just like that," Julie said.

"Was that Robert?" I said.

"Whatsisname is fine," Julie said. "I couldn't even leave Michael until I had Whatsis lined up."

"I like men," I said.

"I do too. But we both need to make sure we like ourselves with a man or without one."

"Wow," I said. "Shrink city."

"It's annoying, isn't it?" Julie said.

"You're trying to help," I said.

"I'm saying maybe you need to get help. A few words of advice from me won't make you change your needs."

"Maybe they will," I said. "You know how competitive I am. Maybe I'll prove you wrong."

Julie smiled. She forgave me my foolishness. "Maybe," she said. "Have you found out anything about Melanie Joan's husband?"

"Dr. Melvin," I said. "Maybe I should go to him about my need for men."

"I wouldn't," Julie said. "Have you learned anything?"

"All his patients seem to be female," I said. "I have names for three days' worth of them."

"Do they help, at all?"

"No. I don't know any of them."

We finished our piña coladas and ordered more.

"All women," Julie said.

"Un huh."

The bar was filling with after-work people keeping an eye out for companionship. They were young.

"If this man is the way he seems to be," Julie said, "and he has a therapeutic practice devoted exclusively to women . . ."

"I don't know that it's exclusive," I said.

"Okay, how about preponderance?"

"Preponderance seems accurate."

"Good," Julie said. "So with all these women available to him, and vulnerable . . ."

"He'd take advantage of that."

"He might. I mean it's hideously inappropriate . . ."

"So is cutting your wrists and smearing the blood on a window."

"Did you report him for that?" Julie said.

"No. Melanie Joan didn't want to."

"Because?"

"Because she didn't want to get into a long scandalous hearing process, she said."

"You believe her?" Julie said.

"That could be a reason," I said. "But he's still got a lot of power over her."

"He would know how to use it," Julie said.

"Because he's a shrink?"

"Sure."

"Well," I said. "Maybe I'll monitor him after hours and see what that turns up."

"And if it turns up something?" Julie said.

I smiled at her. "Jule," I said, "you know I don't know what I'm doing."

"None of us seem to," Julie said. "Are you getting paid to investigate Dr. Melvin?"

"Not exactly."

"So why?"

"Why investigate?"

"Un huh."

"Well, maybe if I could figure him out I could help Melanie Joan get rid of him."

"And thus put yourself out of work."

I shrugged.

"I'm not really suited to bodyguard anyway. I'm a detective."

"But you made an exception for her," Julie said.

"I guess."

"And now that you have, you feel bad for her," Julie said.

"I do."

"Don't get confused," Julie said.

"About what?"

"About where she ends and you begin," Julie said.

"I've been confused about that all my life," I said.

"Well," Julie said. "At least you know it."

We were crowded now, down to the corner of the bar as more and more young people pushed in for a drink.

"It might be even better," I said, "if I could do something about it."

"That would be the next step," Julie said.

"Do you have a suggestion?"

"Maxwell Copeland," Julie said.

"I think a woman shrink would be better."

Julie shook her head.

"Male or female doesn't matter," she said. "Max Copeland is the best psychiatrist on the planet."

"On the planet?"

Julie laughed. "That I know," she said. She took her business card from her purse and wrote a phone number on the back. "Tell him I referred you," she said.

"Have you been his patient?" I said.

"No. I know him too well for him to treat me."

"Funny, isn't it," I said. "For the most intimate help we seek out strangers."

"They are strangers to you," Julie said. "But not to the illness."

"You see me as ill?" I said.

"Don't get worked up over words," Julie said. "I believe that you need to resolve your relationship with Richie."

"Might that not be a relationship rooted in love?"

"It might," Julie said. "But the fact that you can't be with him or without him suggests that there's some pathology involved."

I sat back. I wanted to show her that she was absurd. But I couldn't think of a way to do that, so maybe she wasn't absurd.

"Well," I said. "It's a little startling to see you in action."

"You mean as a therapist?"

"Yes, I guess that's what you're being."

"I'm being your friend," Julie said.
"Yes," I said. "I guess that's what it is."
I took the card.

CHAPTER
SEVENTEEN

I drove Melanie Joan to New York. She and I in the front seat, Rosie in the backseat and somewhat grumpy about it. By Rosie's perception Melanie Joan was in her seat. On the way, somewhere around Greenwich, I asked her if she knew anything about her husband's medical practice.

"He's not my husband anymore," she said.

"True," I said. "What can you tell me about Dr. Melvin's practice?"

"I know he's a Freudian."

"And you know that it's predominantly female."

Melanie Joan smiled. "Women adore him," she said. "I used to."

"Often in psychotherapy the therapist has considerable power over the patient," I said.

"Absolutely," Melanie Joan said.

"Do you think that Dr. Melvin might exploit that power?"

"Absolutely," Melanie Joan said.

The rolling Connecticut countryside along the Merritt Parkway was bright. Indian summer was upon us. Melanie Joan's publisher had offered to rent us a car, but I was happier driving my Subaru wagon, and I knew Rosie preferred it. There was something in the way she had repeated "absolutely".

"How did you meet Dr. Melvin?" I said.

"I was his patient."

"You were in therapy with him?"

"Yes."

"And the marriage grew out of the therapy?" I said.

"It seemed so natural," Melanie Joan said. "To marry my savior."

For maybe the twentieth time since we'd left Boston, Rosie wedged herself up onto the center console and gazed firmly at the front seat where Melanie Joan was sitting.

"Is she dying to come up here?" Melanie Joan said.

"Yes."

"Well, can she sit in my lap?"

"As easily as anything she's ever done before," I said.

Melanie Joan patted the tops of her thighs.

"Come on, Rosie," she said.

Rosie looked at me. I nodded. Rosie jumped from the console onto Melanie Joan's lap.

"Ow," Melanie Joan said.

"You offered," I said.

"I was not planning on an all-out assault," Melanie Joan said.

Rosie worried around on Melanie Joan's lap for a while until she got in just the right position, then settled.

"She thought you'd never ask," I said. "Were you, ah, dating while you were his patient?"

"John preferred to call us clients," Melanie Joan said.

74

I nodded. "Sure. Were you dating?"

"Yes," Melanie Joan said. "Not right away, of course. I was in therapy with him for maybe three months before he suggested we might get together for dinner."

"And?" I said.

"And after the third time we had dinner, we went back to my place and had sex."

"Whose idea was that?" I said.

I was trying to keep my voice neutral.

"At the time I thought it was mine," Melanie Joan said. "I was thrilled when he agreed."

She wasn't looking at me. She was looking out the window while she slowly patted Rosie.

"And now?"

"Now I think he manipulated me into it."

"That would be my guess," I said.

CHAPTER
EIGHTEEN

We were in a two-bedroom suite at the Hotel Carlyle, in the living room having tea and talking with a film producer named Murray Gottlieb. We were also supposed to be talking with a film star named Hal Race, which was why we had come down to New York in the first place, but Hal hadn't showed yet so Melanie Joan and Murray and I were making small talk and eating tea sandwiches while we waited. One of the doormen had volunteered to walk Rosie, and since Rosie would go walking with anyone who asked her, she was out for a while and we could eat our tea sandwiches without interference.

"I talked to Hal's assistant," Gottlieb said. "Just before I came over. She says he knows of the meeting. That it's on his calendar and his PalmPilot."

Melanie Joan smiled pleasantly and nodded.

"Mr. Gottlieb and Mr. Race," she said to me, "are interested in making a feature film . . ."

"Not just one," Gottlieb said. "We see Melanie Joan's work as a franchise."

"Like *Lethal Weapon*," I said. "Or Bruce Willis in a skyscraper."

"Exactly," Gottlieb said. "We're prepared to make a deal."

He seemed pleased at my intelligence.

"And the point of this meeting," Melanie Joan said, "is to see if I like them and want to work with them."

"How's it going so far?" I said to Melanie Joan.

"And Mr. Race hasn't said anything stupid," Melanie Joan said.

"Yet," I said.

"That's right," Melanie Joan said, "yet."

Gottlieb looked as if we'd said something else nice. Someone knocked on the door.

"Oh," Gottlieb said, "that must be Hal, let me get it."

He opened the door and Rosie looked at him and barked. Gottlieb jumped a little. Behind Rosie, at the other end of the leash, was the doorman.

"I've brought Rosie back," he said.

"Oh, boy," Gottlieb said. "What a cute little dog."

The doorman unleashed Rosie and Gottlieb bent down to pat her. She swerved around Gottlieb and dashed to me with her mouth open and her tongue out.

"Let me give you something," I said to the doorman.

Gottlieb took a twenty-dollar bill out and handed it to the doorman.

"Thanks a lot," he said.

The doorman took it with that smooth way doormen have and backed out and closed the door. Gottlieb came back into the living room. Rosie was up on the couch beside me, her ears back, looking at Gottlieb.

"Hi, Rosie," Gottlieb said.

Rosie didn't answer.

"What kind of dog is he?" Gottlieb said.

"She's a miniature English bull terrier," I said.

"Well, he's really cute."

We drank some more tea. I gave Rosie a smoked salmon finger sandwich.

"I love this franchise," Gottlieb said. "Maybe get Julia or Gwyneth to costar with Hal."

"Do you have a writer in mind?" Melanie Joan said.

"Well, if we can't get you . . ."

Melanie Joan shook her head.

". . . then we will absolutely insist on someone who will stay true to your books," Gottlieb said.

Melanie Joan smiled and nodded. Someone knocked at the door. Gottlieb jumped up to answer, and this time it was Hal Race. He was not as tall as I am, with longish black hair and a sort of seductive petulance around his mouth. On-screen he had always looked much taller. He had on baggy jeans and a V-neck black tee shirt and a Harris tweed jacket. A black watch-plaid woolen scarf was wound once around his neck with the long end hanging below his knees. His sunglasses sat up on top of his head nestled among the curls. He was impossibly gorgeous for a guy his size. I smiled without showing it at what Richie would think about him. And Spike, my God, Spike!

"Sorry, sorry, sorry," Hal said.

"No problem, Hal," Gottlieb said.

"I just broke up with my girlfriend last night," Hal said, "and I was so bummed that I spent the night at Romeo's Retreat. My head's really fucked up."

"I'm terribly sorry, Hal," Gottlieb said and introduced Melanie Joan.

Hal made full eye contact, and smiled brilliantly.

"What an honor," he said. "I really love your books."

"This is my friend Sunny Randall," Melanie Joan said.

Hal said, "Hey," and glanced at me briefly and spotted Rosie.

"The dog has got to go," Hal said.

"I'm sure they can put him in the bedroom," Gottlieb said.

"Maybe we could put Hal in the bedroom," I said.

Gottlieb smiled again. "Why don't I just put him away for you, Cindy."

"Sunny," I said. "Perhaps I could just hold her here in my lap and Mr. Race will be safe."

"The dog has to go," Hal said.

Gottlieb looked at Melanie Joan. Melanie Joan smiled back at him and said nothing.

"Here," Gottlieb said, "let me take him for you."

"No."

"Excuse me?"

"You may not touch my dog," I said.

"Hey," Race said, "who is this broad? It's only a fucking dog."

"Like your last movie," I said.

"Perhaps Sunny can hold Rosie on her lap," Melanie Joan said.

"Fuck this," Race said. "I'm walking."

His little face was very red. I took a deep breath. This wasn't my deal. It wouldn't kill Rosie to stay for a while in my bedroom. I could give her one of her chewy toys. I looked at Melanie Joan. Her face was serene. She stood and put out her hand.

"Well, it was very nice to meet you, Mr. Race."

Hal started to put his hand out automatically, and stopped. "Excuse me?"

"You're walking," Melanie Joan said. "I'm saying goodbye."

I could see the slow gears in Hal's head begin to turn. He smiled warmly.

"Hey, Melanie, lighten up," he said. "I was just fooling around."

"You're not walking?"

"No, no. I been up all night and my head's a little screwed. If Cindy holds that dog, I'm sure it'll be fine."

Melanie Joan turned to me and smiled with continuing serenity.

"That okay with you, Cindy?"

"Sure," I said.

Hal didn't actually look at Rosie, but he smiled his warm sincere smile at me.

"He is kind of a cute dog," Hal said.

CHAPTER
NINETEEN

We were shimmying across the hateful steel grid bridge over the Housatonic River, south of New Haven.

"Why in God's name do they make bridges like this?" Melanie Joan said.

"Must have something to do with money," I said.

"Well, aren't you cynical," Melanie Joan said.

"I am," I said.

My car reached solid highway again and settled in. Rosie settled back down on Melanie Joan's lap. And we continued north.

"You put a lot on the line just to keep Rosie from being shut in the bedroom," I said.

Melanie Joan smiled and kissed Rosie on the top of her head. Rosie accepted it as if it were expected and had no reaction beyond a small ear twitch.

"It wasn't a big risk," Melanie Joan said. "He wasn't going to walk."

"Because?"

"Because he needed the money."

"Hal Race needs money?" I said.

"Certainly. He has three alimonies and two child supports. He has a manager, an agent, a driver, a personal assistant, a bodyguard, his own makeup person, his own hair person, a house in Malibu, a ranch in Santa Barbara, four cars . . ."

"Four," I said.

"Four," Melanie Joan said. "Then there's his retinue."

"Retinue?"

"The people he hangs around with."

"They cost money?"

"Of course. He always picks up the tab, dinner, plane fare, whatever."

"They don't hang with him because they like him?" I said.

"Would you?" Melanie Joan said.

"No."

"See?"

"So he needed the money too badly to walk out on your deal."

"Of course. It's a good deal. We already have some foreign money in place. The studio's committed to a big-budget picture and he gets a percentage of the adjusted gross."

"What the hell is adjusted gross?" I said.

"No one knows," Melanie Joan said. "Only the really heavy hitters, you know, Harrison Ford maybe, Tom Cruise, Russell Crowe, Julia Roberts, get a piece of the unadjusted gross. And even their percentage of the gross is probably doctored by the studio."

"Legally?" I said.

"No."

"I'm shocked," I said. "Shocked, I tell you."

"So poor Hal grows up thinking he matters," Melanie Joan said. "Everybody he ever talks to says he's great, really great. They say that they loved his last picture, absolutely loved it. They say he's got authentic star power, that he's the man, that the camera is kind to him, that every idea he has is great."

"And he believes it?"

"On the set, every time the camera stops rolling he sits in a chair with his name on it and somebody comes around with a hand mirror hanging on a string around their neck and they make sure his hair is perfect and retouch his makeup and hold up the mirror and say "You look fabulous." "

"Movie-star land," I said.

"Yes," Melanie Joan said. "And as long as he stays in it and doesn't venture out, he can believe all of it."

"And when he threatened to walk and you said go ahead, it was like somebody left the door open for a minute and he felt the chill of reality."

"A momentary breeze from human land," Melanie Joan said.

"So how is it," I said, "that you can be so tough with Hal Race, and so, ah, hesitant, with your ex-husband?"

"Hal Race is a harmless turd," Melanie Joan said.

"And Dr. Melvin?"

"He's not harmless," Melanie Joan said.

CHAPTER
TWENTY

That afternoon I called Dr. Melvin's service and was told that his office hours were 8a.m. to 4p.m. That night after office hours, I sat in my car up the street from John Melvin's home and office, in the shadowy patch between two streetlights. I wanted to see how Dr. Melvin spent his evenings. Rosie was asleep on the front seat beside me, making small satisfied snorey noises. Her left foreleg was over her nose.

My motor was idling and I was listening to a new CD Spike had given me in which Peter Marshall sang the great songs of my father's boyhood. I liked the music of my father's boyhood. Probably Oedipal.

A gray Lexus sedan pulled up across the street in front of John Melvin's house and a slim blond woman got out wearing an ankle-length black coat. She went up the windy little path and into Melvin's house. It was too dark to be sure, but she could have been someone I'd seen before. I checked my list of license-plate numbers and found a match for the Lexus. The owner's name was Augustus J. Walsh, and he lived in Winchester. The blond woman was in there for an hour and twenty minutes. She came back down the path walking fast, got in her car, and pulled away fast. At

8:15 a silver Volvo wagon pulled up and another woman got out. She wore jeans and a fur jacket. Her hair was dark and she had a young walk as she went up to Melvin's house. I checked the Volvo. Another match. This time the car was registered to Kim Crawford in Concord. I listened to Peter Marshall some more . . . *crazy moon . . . I thought about you . . . everything happens to me*. Rosie shifted sides once, so that her right foreleg was over her nose. She made some sort of snorty sound which was, I believe bullterrier for snoring. Nobody else showed up at Dr. Melvin's house. At twenty past ten, Kim came out and walked to the Volvo. It was early November and the nearly half moon looked paler and colder and more uninvolved than I remembered it looking in the summer. At eleven, two white men, neither of them Melvin, both about his age, came out of the house and walked up the street a ways to a black Porsche Boxster parked away from the streetlight. The plate numbers didn't match any that I had. They could still be patients, of course, but if they were patients, would they come together? Couples therapy? And what were they doing while the women were there, or what were the women doing while they were there, quartet therapy? The Boxster pulled slowly out of the shadows and proceeded up the block and turned left and disappeared.

Nobody else showed up for a late-hour appointment with Dr. Melvin. Dr. Melvin did not come out or go anywhere. A woman about my mother's age walked by with some sort of spaniel on a leash. Rosie sprang from slumber and gargled savagely at it and bounced around

85

off the inside of the car. The woman looked offended and pulled the spaniel away from the car briskly. When the spaniel was out of range Rosie stood trembling alertly for another minute and then went back to sleep. Nothing else happened. I stayed grimly put for another hour and fifteen minutes, and, at twenty-five to twelve I quit and drove home to South Boston.

CHAPTER
TWENTY-ONE

I went to see Max Copeland.

"I'm a detective," I said. "I'm working on a case involving a psychiatrist and I thought it might be useful if I had someone like you to consult with on it. My friend Julie recommended you."

Copeland nodded. "Yes," he said. "I've spoken with Julie."

He had very clear features and a strong neck. His black hair was combed back smooth. He wore round eyeglasses with black frames.

"What do you think?" I said. "Could we work together?"

"Who is the psychiatrist?" Copeland said.

"I prefer not to say."

"Because?"

"Until I've made my case," I said, "I feel that I should not, ah, bad-mouth him to his colleagues."

"Because?"

"Well," I said, "I don't want you prejudging him."

"And you don't trust me to make that decision?"

"Why are we even discussing this," I said. "What difference does it make?"

Copeland leaned back in his chair. He was wearing a black suit with a white shirt and a pink satin tie. He put his hands together, fingertips touching, and tapped his upper lip.

"At the heart of any therapeutic relationship is trust. If we are to get anywhere in here I have to trust you that you are speaking truthfully and you have to trust me that I can handle it."

"I'm not here for therapy," I said.

Copeland made one of those little nonjudgmental head gestures that shrinks seem to have patented, and didn't say anything.

"He, call him Dr. Ex, is stalking his former wife. I thought if I went to see him and pretended to need therapy, I might be able to get a handle on what he's about."

"And?"

"And find a way to chase him off."

"And you have no emotional stake in this," Copeland said.

"That's right," I said.

Copeland was beginning to annoy me.

"But you'd like to solve the case."

"Sure," I said. "I like Mrs. Ex. It would please me to be able to help her."

"That's all?"

"I'm a detective," I said. "It's the kind of thing people hire me to do. I would feel good about a job well done."

"Of course," he said. "Are you married?"

"I'm divorced," I said.

"Children?"

"No. What difference does it make?"

"I don't know," Copeland said. "It's why I'm asking."

"Well, it doesn't make a difference."

"Does it annoy you that I ask?" Copeland said.

"No. It just seems irrelevant."

"What would be relevant?"

"Jesus, you are being a pain in the ass," I said.

Copeland smiled and made no comment.

"Here's the plan," I said. "I'm going to go see Dr. Ex as a patient. I believe that he exploits his women patients, and I want to see if he'll try to exploit me. So I thought I'd go and talk with him and then come to you and tell you what happened and see what you thought."

Copeland nodded.

"Will you agree to that?"

"Yes."

"Okay," I said. "I'm not seeing you for my health, so to pay you through health insurance would be fraudulent. If you could bill me direct you could be paid out of my expense account."

Copeland nodded.

"You don't talk very much," I said.

Copeland smiled again. "When Freud spoke of the talking cure," Copeland said, "he was not referring to the therapist."

"Okay," I said. "If you want to pretend it's therapy, we'll pretend it's therapy, as long as I can get your input on Dr. Ex."

Copeland nodded.

"Assuming he's a man who exploits his female patients," I said, "what kind of story should I tell him?"

"It is simpler to talk about things that bother you, and follow where it leads," Copeland said. "Then you don't have to maintain a fiction."

"So what do I say when I first go in and sit down?"

"Relax, pay attention to your feelings, see what comes."

"Don't prepare?" I said.

"I wouldn't," Copeland said. "Be genuine. There are things that bother you, let them lead you."

"And if things don't bother me?"

"Then you are not human," Copeland said.

CHAPTER
TWENTY-TWO

I was at the gym with Spike.

"You do everything I do," he said, "and maybe someday you'll look just like me."

He was hitting the big body bag, the sweat soaked through his gray sweatshirt.

"You look like a polar bear," I said.

"So?"

"So how will looking like a polar bear enhance my sex life?"

"Hasn't hurt mine," Spike said.

"And we're both trying to access the same gender pool," I said.

"See?"

"Let me try that," I said.

Spike stepped away from the bag and gave me access. I assessed the bag. When I was small my father had showed me how to hit it, despite my mother's persistent disapproval. But it was a long time ago, and I was, after all, a girl.

"Put the gloves on," Spike said, "or you skin your knuckles up."

Spike's gloves were too big. I turned my fists in a little and hit the bag with a left hand like Daddy had taught me. The bag shook only a little.

"Where's Billy Banks when you need him," Spike said.

"What am I doing wrong?"

"Nothing," Spike said. "You're a girl. Girls can't hit the heavy bag."

"And that would be why?" I said.

"You're missing a crucial part of the anatomy," Spike said.

"You don't hit it with that," I said.

"No, but it guides the punches."

I hit the bag again.

"You need to hit it as much as you can with the weight of your cute, puny body behind it," Spike said. "Like this."

He hit the bag bare-fisted. It jumped.

"See, keep your hands in close. Turn your shoulder in, now, try to punch through the bag."

I did what he said.

"Better," he said. "But you need to try to punch through it. You're landing the punches on the surface."

I did it again. The bag moved.

"See?" Spike said.

"I made it jump," I said

"You made it sway," Spike said.

"I'm a girl," I said. "Girls like to make it sway."

"That's 'cause you can't make it jump."

"I could make it jump if I wanted to."

Spike grinned at me. "Sunny," he said, "you could make me jump if you wanted to."

"I know," I said.

The gym was busy. I'd been going there for ten years, since before my divorce, and I recognized a lot of the people. They were there every time I was, working hard. A lot of them, especially the women, had trainers. The trainers were very serious about it. And almost everybody looked exactly the same as they had ten years ago, except older. Maybe it was all only about health.

When we got through, Spike and I sat in the lounge and had some juice.

"I told you about Melanie Joan Hall's husband."

"The stalker?"

"Yes. He's a shrink."

"Maybe he can help himself understand why he's stalking her," Spike said.

"I'm going to go see him."

"About you and Richie?"

"I think he's exploiting women patients," I said to Spike.

"Doesn't make him a bad shrink," Spike said.

"I'm going to go in and start therapy with him and see if I can catch him."

"And then what?"

"Then I've got some leverage on him," I said. "To get him off Melanie Joan's case."

"Two birds with one stone," Spike said. "You could squeeze in a little therapy while you were in there."

"Oh stop it," I said. "I went to another psychiatrist, a doctor named Copeland that Julie sent me to, to get some help with my presenting symptoms."

A tall young man with big blue eyes walked by in a tank top undershirt. He was in great shape.

"Yowzah!" Spike said, watching him pass.

"Me too," I said. "Copeland said to stick as close as I could to the truth and that way I wouldn't have to make stuff up."

"You like him?" Spike said. "Copeland?"

"Yes. I think so. Except he keeps treating me as if I were a candidate for therapy."

"Well, heaven for-fucking-fend," Spike said.

"You think I need therapy? I had some when Richie and I separated."

"And that straightened you right out," Spike said.

"Yes."

"Other than you can't be with Richie or without him," Spike said.

"Oh pooh," I said, "to you. Nothing wrong with a little ambivalence."

"Yeah," Spike said. "There is."

CHAPTER
TWENTY-THREE

I sat in Dr. John Melvin's office, looking like a perfect doofus in pale lip gloss, a black wig, wraparound sunglasses, and one of those adorable hats that models wear in magazine ads, where the brim turns up in the front. The hat solidified the doofus look. But Melvin had seen me in my natural stunning blonde mode, so silly as I felt, a disguise seemed sensible. *Sunny Randall, woman of a thousand faces*. I was using my real first name and my former married name. I was Sonya Burke.

Melvin sat sideways at his desk wearing charcoal slacks and cordovan shoes, a blue blazer, a blue and red striped tie, and a blue shirt.

"Would you care to remove your glasses?" Dr. Melvin said.

I sat on the edge of my chair with my knees together and my hands folded in my lap. I shook my head.

"It is often useful," he said, "for the therapist to see the patient's eyes."

Still sitting stiffly, I shook my head again and looked down at my folded hands. I wasn't as ill at ease as I looked, but I was more ill at ease than I had expected to be.

"Of course," he said. "Whatever is comfortable."

Neither of us said anything for a little while. If it made Melvin uncomfortable, he didn't show it. I shifted a little in my chair. I wasn't acting. I was uncomfortable. Which was odd. I've done undercover work before. I had certainly dealt with more dangerous people than John Melvin, M.D.

I had on jeans and tan hiking boots and a black tee shirt. I had bought a shapeless, loose-fitting hip-length black wool jacket to complement my hat and wig, and I wore my gun near the small of my back under the coat.

"I'm divorced," I said.

Melvin cocked his head a little as if that were interesting.

"Oh?" he said.

I was quiet. He was quiet.

After a while Melvin said, "How do you feel about being divorced?"

"Sad."

"What makes you sad?"

I looked at him.

"Being divorced," I said.

"What about being divorced?"

"Excuse me?"

I felt some annoyance. Couldn't this jerk understand English?

"What about the divorce makes you sad?"

"I miss Richie," I said.

Melvin nodded again and leaned back a little in his swivel chair and leaned his chin into his half-closed right hand. The room was very quiet.

"I've dated a lot of other men, and I've liked them, I've liked some of them very much."

I could hear no cars passing. No leaf blowers blowing, no dogs barking, no water running. The stillness was a little daunting. Melvin blended right into it.

"But I never loved any of them," I said. "Enough."

"Enough to sleep with?" Melvin said.

His eyes were recessed and dark and I could almost feel them resting on me.

"Yes."

"But not enough to marry."

"No."

Melvin kept his eyes on me, his chin on his hand. I was aware of my own breathing.

"Tell me about the divorce," Melvin said after a while.

"We kept . . . I don't know exactly. We couldn't live together. We kept trying to fix each other."

"Were you compatible sexually?"

"Yes."

"Do you still see one another?"

"Yes. Actually we get along much better than when we were married."

"Are you still intimate?"

"Occasionally," I said.

Melvin nodded again and waited. He seemed as if he could wait comfortably for the full fifty minutes. I almost smiled. I wondered what would happen if I sat silent for the entire session.

"Whose idea is that?"

"I suppose it's mutual," I said.

"That's always best," he said.

I thought for a moment I saw something flicker in his face. Then it was gone. The session ended and I went back to my car feeling odd and a little light-headed. Who was investigating whom?

CHAPTER
TWENTY-FOUR

"Are you prepared to fly?" Melanie Joan asked me.

"Yes."

"And you're not afraid? After September eleventh?"

"I was afraid before September eleventh," I said.

"I know," Melanie Joan said. "I am too, but I can't live the life I lead if I don't fly."

I nodded.

"They want us to come to LA for meetings," Melanie Joan said.

"They?"

"Murray and Hal, they're trying to sell the project."

"Sell it?"

"Yes."

"I thought you had already sold it to them."

"I agreed to be partners with them," Melanie Joan said. "So they don't have to buy the rights."

I had the feeling that she thought it amazing that I knew so little about filmmaking.

"But we still need financing and distribution," Melanie Joan said.

"So you have meetings with people who can do that," I said.

"And we pitch them the project," Melanie Joan said.

I nodded. "Which is why they call it . . ."

"A pitch meeting," we said in unison.

Even I had heard of pitch meetings.

"And you think Melvin will follow you out there?"

"He may, I don't know. In any event I'd like you with me."

"Because I'm such a good time?" I said.

"Because there's something about you that makes me braver."

"Really?" I said.

"Yes."

"That's very nice," I said.

"It's not meant to be nice," Melanie Joan said. "It's simply the truth."

"Well," I said. "I wish it were working better for me."

"Nonsense," Melanie Joan said.

"Nonsense?"

"I know you are being wry and self-effacing," Melanie Joan said. "But you know perfectly well the things you're capable of, and bravery is one of them. You are slim and cute and tougher than a boiled shoe."

"You understand me that well?" I said.

I wasn't sure she knew me well enough to have that much confidence in her judgment of me, even if it was flattering.

"I can't write," Melanie Joan said. "But I can think."

"Damn," I said. "You do Melanie Joan so well that sometimes I forget there's someone else inside there."

Melanie Joan inclined her head and accepted her due.

"I don't miss all that much," she said.

We were having dinner in a new restaurant called Blu in the new Sports Club/LA that had gone up on the corner of Tremont and Boylston.

"So why don't they call this Sports Club/Boston?" I said.

"It would lack panache," Melanie Joan said. "Will you fly with me to Los Angeles?"

"Yes."

CHAPTER
TWENTY-FIVE

Brian Kelly called me while I was in the initial planning stage of packing.

"DMV says that the owner of the Porsche Boxster you were looking at is Dirk Beals, lives in Boston on Mt. Vernon Street."

"That's locked right into the computer," I said.

"You using computers now," Kelly said.

"I was referring to my brain," I said.

"Oh, sorry, I forgot about your brain."

"Well, don't," I said.

"It's just that I was interested in accessing other, ah, facets of your self."

"And, as a I recall," I said, "you succeeded."

"Was it good for you, too?"

"Oh shut up," I said. "Thanks for the help with DMV."

As I hung up I could hear Kelly chuckling.

My clothes were organized in carefully laid-out categories, on hangers, spread on the bed, over the backs of chairs. Rosie lay among them with her nose on her paws and her eyes that looked like watermelon seeds moving as I moved. She always watched me like that. I knew it was because she loved me, and I knew it was also because there was always a chance that I might find a ball and throw it for her. Love is rarely unadulterated.

Packing was one of the several things about me Richie never understood. He thought packing meant putting his shaving kit in a carry-on suitcase, along with some clean shirts and underwear. I was mostly packed when I had decided what to bring. Putting the actual selections into an actual suitcase was only a finishing flourish. The weather in LA this day and the day before had been in the high seventies and sunny. It could rain, of course. And sometimes, I knew, when it was dark and rainy it could be a little chilly. I shuffled some outerwear around. We might eat out in elegant restaurants, but, as best I could remember, elegant restaurants in LA did not evoke elegant attire. Except for some. And I had to give serious thought to what one wore to a pitch meeting, when one was, more or less, only the bodyguard.

Mt. Vernon Street was the kind of address where you would expect to run into someone named Dirk Beals, who drove a Boxster. When I got back from LA I could go and sit outside his house for a while. Sooner or later, as my father had taught me, you learn something.

I was finally down to the decision between black leather pants and a charcoal skirt and jacket. I stared at them. Rosie stared at me. I took in some air and finally, sadly, took the skirt and jacket to my closet and hung them back up. I hoped I wasn't making a mistake.

In the morning after I had gone, Richie would come and pick Rosie up. I went to the kitchen counter to write him a note. I knew he knew how to take care of Rosie. He used to live with Rosie and me. But I had to write a note every time and remind him of what she ate and when and how much and who the vet was and where I could be reached in an emergency. One of the compulsions of motherhood. I had a glass of wine while I wrote the note. While I sipped my wine I wrote out carefully which ball Rosie most liked to chase, and when was the best time to take her out, and not to let her chase her tail too much, and what day I'd be back for her.

When I was done I poured another glass of wine. I reread the note. Then I got up and took my wineglass and walked down the loft to where my easel was set up under the skylight, where it caught the sunlight in the morning. I was painting the Weeks Footbridge, and I was maybe half done. Maybe the brushlines needed to be coarser. I drank some more wine and looked at my painting for a while. It was still incomplete, but it was coming.

Writing the note to Richie about shared custody of Rosie wasn't just compulsive motherhood. I knew it was also a simulation of connected domesticity. I was re-creating something that may never have been.

And might never be.

Or might.

CHAPTER
TWENTY-SIX

Melanie Joan's West Coast agent, Tony Gault, joined us at Buckboard Productions on the Paramount lot, watching, with a hint of amusement, I thought, through small eyeglasses with round black frames. He was tall and slim with a sort of sharp face, wearing pressed jeans and a gray cashmere tee shirt under a black cashmere jacket. His dark hair was thick, slightly longer than most. When he ran a hand through it, which, I noticed, he did frequently, the wave fell right back in place. Every woman I've ever known would kill someone to get hair like that. Tony Gault seemed to take it for granted.

Tony and I were at opposite ends of a semicircle which also included Hal Race, Murray Gottlieb, and Melanie Joan. Sitting on a couch to one side of us, with her shoes off and her legs tucked up under her, was a slightly plump young woman named Mandy, and, at the epicenter of all this, seated in a wing chair at the center of all attention, was a kid named Cash Resnick.

"Cash and I really love your work," Mandy was saying. "When we heard you were coming in we were very excited. Everybody was, around here."

Cash's adolescent face showed no emotion. I wondered if he shaved yet. Maybe he was old enough, his hair was receding. He wore what was left slicked straight back smooth against his small skull, and gathered into something that looked like the tail from a very small pony. He wore an NYPD tee shirt and pale blue jeans that he had apparently put on straight from the dryer. There were even a couple of small carefully tattered holes. For footwear he wore some elaborate running shoes.

"Would you care for something to drink?" Mandy said. "Coffee? Soft drink? Water?"

None of us did. Mandy looked at Cash. Cash nodded slightly. His youth fascinated me. If he shaved, how come his sideburns didn't square off?

"Well," Mandy said, "perhaps you'd like to tell us why you're here?"

"Well," Hal Race said, "as most people know, I've been a big fan of Melanie's work since day one. And when *Vagabond Heart* came out I knew I had to play Aaron Lassiter."

Resnick sat in blank immobility. It was as if Hal Race had not spoken. Hal Race glanced at Mandy and she smiled and nodded. Desperate to hear more.

"So I got ahold of Murray, and he got ahold of Tony, and we lucked out. Melanie said yes. And here we are."

No one said anything. I saw Tony Gault looking at me across the silent half circle. His eyes looked as if he might be smiling. I met his look. Wasn't this hideous. Cash continued to sit and contemplate eternity. Maybe he had died and they didn't want us to know.

"Maybe you could tell us a little of the story," Mandy said.

"Sure would," Hal said. "And Melanie, you jump in anywhere if you think I'm getting it wrong."

"I will," Melanie Joan said.

"Okay. Aaron Lassiter is the president of a fabulously successful international private security firm and comes home to find his wife of six months, Heather, has disappeared. I see maybe Gwyneth, but it might be the place to cast an unknown, do a little star making, so to speak."

Cash was passionately unaffected by all of this. Mandy nodded vigorously. She was delighted.

"So Lassiter turns out the full resources of his security agency to find Heather . . ."

I had read the book, and I had sat through the rehearsal in our suite at the Beverly Wilshire, while Melanie Joan and Gottlieb and Hal shaped the pitch. I looked at Tony Gault again. He seemed composed and something more, maybe the tilt of his head, something suggested that he found everything amusing. I crossed my eyes at him. He winked. Hal's pitch finally wound down, with Cash continuing in deep catatonia.

Mandy said, "That's great. The title might have to be changed. Warners did a film a couple of years ago called *Vagabond*, and it tanked badly."

"What's in a name?" Hal said.

Cash spoke.

"You have a script?" he said.

From the sound of his voice he might never shave. Hal Race looked at Gottlieb.

"We're hoping you'll commission one," Gottlieb said.

Cash didn't say anything else.

"Well, damn, look at the time. Cash has another meeting at two. This sounds very exciting. Let us think on it and talk, and we'll get back to you. Call you, Murray? Or Tony."

"Either one would be fine," Gottlieb said.

Cash stood and turned and left the office. Mandy got up and held the door open and smiled at us as we trooped out.

CHAPTER
TWENTY-SEVEN

Hal, being a movie star, was too important to go, and Gottlieb had another pitch. But Melanie Joan and Tony Gault and I went across Melrose Avenue to a Mexican place called Lucy's El Adobe to have lunch and debrief. It wasn't crowded at 2:15 in the afternoon and we got a big booth for ourselves.

"The margaritas are to die for," Tony said. "Shall we get a pitcher?"

"I may need a pitcher just for me," Melanie Joan said.

The walls of Lucy's were covered with celebrity photographs.

"Who's that guy?" I said.

"That's Bill Strout, old CBS newsman."

"No, the guy with him. He looks familiar."

Tony studied the picture for a minute.

"No idea," he said.

The margaritas came. I had a small sip of one. It was to die for.

"Good pitch," Tony said.

"We didn't say anything," Melanie Joan said. "Except Hal giving a plot summary."

"That's probably the best approach," Tony said.

"And for God's sake what is it with the stone face on that little twerp in the tee shirt."

"That's his pitch style. He wants people to think he's formidable."

"Formidable?" I said.

Tony smiled again.

"My ex-husband would fall laughing to the ground at the very sight of him," I said.

"Not if he were trying to sell a project," Tony said.

"Even if he were."

"Ex-husband," Tony said.

"Yes."

"Tony's not married either," Melanie Joan said.

"That makes three of us," I said.

Lunch came, and pretty soon another pitcher of margaritas.

"Tony used to be married," Melanie Joan said.

"God bless the past tense," Tony said.

If the margaritas were having an effect on him, I couldn't see it. They were having an effect on me. And I liked it.

"You're divorced?" I said.

"From a Southern California film-business bubblehead," Tony said.

"Whom you once thought well enough of to marry."

Tony grinned. "That's because I too am a Southern California film-business bubblehead," he said.

"But cute," Melanie Joan said.

"Oh, yes," Tony said. "Very cute."

"So what will be the next step, ah, pitch wise," I said.

"We see Grady Wilson at Universal, tomorrow at ten."

"No," I said. "I meant this one that we just did."

"Oh." Melanie Joan shrugged. "Probably nothing."

"No need to be negative here," Tony said.

"After a lovely chat with Resnick?" Melanie Joan said. "And Mandy chirp chirp? It would depress a mortician."

"What was Mandy's last name?" I said.

"Mandy," Tony said, and we laughed.

"Seriously, now what happens at Paramount?"

"Seriously?" Tony said. "You're in the wrong business for seriously. Resnick will either have Mandy call me tomorrow and tell us they pass, or he'll buck it along to Sam Kramer."

"Who, in a few days, will have somebody call Tony to tell him they pass."

"Melanie Joan," Tony said, "movies do get made."

"What would you say the percentage was?" Melanie Joan said.

She probably was feeling the effects of the margaritas. She looked like I felt. Tony smiled at her, and me.

"Let's not go there," he said.

"If he passes it along to this Sam Kramer guy," I said, "whoever he is. Does that mean he endorses it?"

Tony laughed. "Not bloody likely," he said. "Sam is head of production. Resnick will buck it along to Sam, with a note saying that, with the right director, and the right screenplay, properly cast, if we had the right budget, this property might be one on which we could consider going forward."

"Daring," I said.

"And Sam can green-light a project?"

"Or not," Tony said.

CHAPTER
TWENTY-EIGHT

Tony Gault dropped us off in front of the Beverly Wilshire and promised to pick us up at nine the next morning.

"I need a nap," Melanie Joan said as we walked through the high lobby. We were staying in front, in the original part of the hotel.

"Margaritas at lunch," I said. "This could screw up our sleep patterns for days." I rang for the elevator.

"Resnick would drive Carrie Nation to drink," Melanie Joan said.

The elevator door opened silently and we stepped in. I pressed five for our floor. As the door started to close a man outside stopped it with his hand and stepped into the elevator, and smiled at us and pushed the CLOSE DOOR button. It was John Melvin. The doors closed. He looked at the lighted button at floor five and smiled at us. I moved my shoulder bag around in front of me and unzipped it.

Melanie Joan seemed to contract. I moved a little so I was fully between her and Melvin, and slid my hand into my unzipped purse. Melvin was wearing white slacks and a raspberry blazer over a white silk tee shirt. His sunglasses were on the top of his head. His hair was

113

perfectly brushed, his skin clear and tanned. He seemed large. The elevator seemed small.

"Hello, ladies," Melvin said.

Melanie Joan was tight into the corner of the elevator behind me. She made a little squeaky sound. Melvin looked at her over my shoulder. His eyes were dark and deep. He seemed to be looking entirely at Melanie Joan, as if I weren't there.

"Isn't this a piece of serendipity," he said.

"I'm going to have to do something about you pretty soon," I said.

His gaze shifted from Melanie Joan and settled onto me like something tangible. He didn't seem to connect me with his doofus new therapy patient who wouldn't remove her sunglasses.

"Or," he said, "vice versa."

The elevator stopped. The doors opened. Without taking my eyes off Melvin, and with my right hand on my gun, I moved Melanie Joan toward the elevator door and followed her out. Melvin stared at both of us as the elevator doors slowly slid shut between us. I watched the arrow on the floor indicator, but it told me nothing. The elevator simply went back down to the lobby.

Behind me Melanie Joan made that little squeak again. I turned.

"You're going to be fine," I said.

"I have to throw up," she said.

"Hang on," I said, "until we get to the room."

She managed to do that. While she was in the bathroom I called down to the desk and asked to be connected to Dr. John Melvin's room. The front desk told me he was not registered at the hotel. I hung up. There was quiet in the bathroom. I went to the door.

"Are you all right?" I said.

"No."

"Do you need me to come in?" I said.

"No."

I was quiet, listening, I heard the water running in the sink.

"Melanie Joan?" I said.

Her voice was hoarse and shaky. "What?"

"I will not," I said, "I *will not* let him hurt you."

She didn't answer.

CHAPTER
TWENTY-NINE

We sat in the suite's living room now with an LA sheriff's deputy who had come over from the substation on San Vicente.

"There is a restraining order on Dr. Melvin," I said.

"In Massachusetts," he said.

He was young and blond with a thick mustache. His arms bulged under the short sleeves of his uniform shirt. He wore his gun high on his right side.

"Yes," I said. "But I assume you honor that."

"Probably do," the deputy said. "I'll need to check."

Melanie Joan had gotten her makeup back intact and combed her hair. But her eyes still hinted red, and her face seemed tight against her skull.

"Can you arrest him?" she said.

Her voice was small and hoarse.

"Once we got our facts in place," the deputy said, "we might be able to do that."

"What facts?" Melanie Joan said.

She was hard to hear, and the deputy leaned toward her as she spoke.

"That there is a restraining order," he said. "That we do honor them from Massachusetts. That he is stalking you."

116

"Why would we make it up?" Melanie Joan said.

"I'm sure you wouldn't, ma'am, but we still have to check."

"Ask her," Melanie Joan said, and nodded at me.

The deputy said, "Yes, ma'am," and looked at me. "You talk with hotel security?"

"Yes."

"He registered here?"

"Not under his name," I said. "They told me they require credit card or other ID when a guest registers."

"And certainly nobody ever fakes it," the deputy said.

"Fake?" I said. "Here in Los Angeles?"

The deputy grinned. "I know the security guy here," the deputy said. "I'll speak to him, have him put a man in the hall."

"Thanks," I said.

The deputy looked at Melanie Joan. "This guy dangerous?" he said.

"Yes."

"He ever try to hurt you physically?"

"Not yet."

"Maybe he won't," the deputy said.

Melanie Joan was silent. The deputy looked at me. "You got a gun?" he said.

"I'm not licensed in California," I said.

"Sure," he said.

"Can you arrest him?" Melanie Joan said again in her small voice.

"If he violates a valid restraining order and we are reciprocal, then yeah, we can arrest him," the deputy said.

He took a card out of his pocket and handed it to me.

"He bothers you again, call me. Meanwhile I'll check out the restraining order."

"Does that mean he has to make another attempt on me before you can do anything?" Melanie Joan said.

"Be nice to catch him doing it," the deputy said.

"And then you'll arrest him?" Melanie Joan said.

"You bet," he said and grinned at me again. "Probably slam him up against a cinder block wall two or three times while we're doing it."

"That would be nice," I said.

CHAPTER
THIRTY

After the deputy left I looked at his card. His name was Raymond Black. I put the card in my purse. I turned back to the room and sat across from Melanie Joan on the couch.

"He terrifies you," I said.

She nodded.

"Other people don't," I said.

She nodded.

"What is it about him?"

She shook her head.

"Has he hurt you? Physically?"

She shook her head.

"But you're afraid he might."

"I'm afraid he'll get me," she said.

"Get you how?"

She shook her head.

"Get me," she said.

"Since I've been with you," I said, "he has made no effort to hurt you."

"He's trying to get me."

"To frighten you?"

She shrugged.

"What does he want from you?" I said.

She was quiet, as if I hadn't spoken. I waited. She stared across the room as if she could see through the wall.

"Do you know what he wants?" I said.

She nodded. I waited some more. She didn't speak, or look at me, or move.

"Melanie Joan," I said. "Look at me."

She kept staring through the wall.

"Look at me," I said.

She turned her head. Her eyes were unfocused, her pupils very big.

"What does he want from you?" I said.

"Submission," she whispered.

I leaned forward to hear better.

"Talk about that," I said.

She shook her head.

"Melanie Joan," I said. "You need to be able to talk about this."

"You are not my shrink," she whispered.

"Do you have one?"

She shook her head.

"Don't you think you ought to?"

She didn't answer.

"I know a wonderful psychiatrist," I said.

She didn't say anything. She simply sat, unmoving, looking back through the wall again. She began to cry, tears on her blank face. She stood suddenly and turned and walked to her bedroom.

"I'll be here," I said. "Right here."

She didn't say anything. She went into the bedroom and closed the door behind her.

My God, what has he done to her?

I went and opened the suite door a crack with the chain still on. I could see a hotel security man standing at the end wall of the hallway. One point for Ray Black.

Then I went to bed and slept with my gun on the night table.

CHAPTER
THIRTY-ONE

"I'm sorry about last night," Melanie Joan said.

We were having breakfast in the dining room, in a window bay that gave us a view of the carport.

"Did you sleep?" I said.

"I took two Ambien," she said.

"That's a good idea," I said.

"You've tried it?"

"There have been nights," I said, "when I couldn't sleep."

"I'm not going to let him do this to me," Melanie Joan said.

"Frighten you?" I said.

"I will not let him reduce me to what I was last night."

"Can you talk about it?"

"No."

"If you ever want to," I said, "I'd like to listen."

"I know."

I drank my orange juice.

"I think Tony is smitten with you," Melanie Joan said.

"Tony Gault?"

"Un huh."

"What makes you think so?"

"I can tell."

"Really?" I said.

Melanie Joan smiled. "Really."

"Well," I said. "He seems quite nice."

"He is," Melanie Joan said. "I mean he's a Hollywood agent, of course."

"And that makes him suspect," I said.

"It does. But I like him."

"Well," I said. "Let's not discourage any advances he might attempt."

"Tony is picking us up at nine. To go to Universal."

"Is the dress code still the same?" I said.

"Yes. Just like yesterday. We dress up in a dressed-down way."

"Perfect," I said.

We drove down to Culver City in Tony Gault's BMW.

"This is the old MGM lot," Tony said as we picked up a drive-on pass at the gate. "That's the Irving Thalberg building over there. Hal and Murray will meet us in Grady's office. Which used to belong to Louis B. Mayer."

I never did quite know who Grady was, or the woman named Alice that was with him. I had stopped paying attention to the pitch. But I'd have to be a more sophisticated girl than I am not to be impressed sitting in Louis B. Mayer's office.

On the drive back to Beverly Hills, Melanie sat up front with Tony and I sat in the backseat. Tony asked us to dinner.

"You go," Melanie Joan said to me. "I'd really rather have a little room service and watch something really awful on television."

"You'll have a wide choice," Tony said.

"I can't leave you alone," I said to Melanie.

"You can. I'll lock my door. There's the lovely hotel security man in the hall. I'll be fine."

"You weren't fine yesterday," I said.

Tony looked at us, and went back to his driving, and said nothing.

"I told you," Melanie Joan said. "I will not let him do that to me again. You need to give me a chance to prove it to myself."

"By leaving you alone."

"Yes."

"I could leave you my gun," I said.

Tony, with his eyes still on the road, said, "Yikes!"

Melanie Joan was half-turned in the front seat, talking to me. She shook her head violently.

"Oh God, no," she said. "I'd be more afraid of the gun than I would be of the evil one."

"No reason to be," I said.

"I won't touch a gun," Melanie said.

A lot of women were like that. It was as if the gun were alive and might fire itself at any minute, killing everyone within range. I knew that guns untouched were inert. For me a gun was a way to equalize disparities in strength and size. Guns could protect people. Me included. If used badly they could be deadly. But that was true of automobiles and scotch whiskey.

124

"I assume all of this is none of my business," Tony said as we waited for the light on Olympic Boulevard. "Sunny will tell you at dinner," Melanie Joan said.

CHAPTER
THIRTY-TWO

We had dined at Spago on North Cañon Drive, and Tony had spoken to half a dozen celebrities including Magic Johnson and Jon Bon Jovi. We had drunk cocktails before dinner, and wine with dinner, and neither of us probably needed the Baileys Irish Cream over ice that we were now sipping in the bar of the Beverly Wilshire at 11:20. But we liked it anyway.

"Are stalkers usually dangerous?" Tony said.

"John Melvin is certainly dangerous in some way to Melanie Joan."

"Physically?"

"I don't know. Being stalked puts you in danger. Being terrified by someone is dangerous. The question is not will he do something. He's already doing something."

Tony nodded. "Whether or not he ever touches her," he said.

"He is touching her, in a manner of speaking."

"Yes. I see that," Tony said. "Can he be arrested?"

"In theory, if he violates a restraining order, he can be arrested. In practice stalkers get a lot of second and third chances. Particularly former husbands. A lot of judges see it as a domestic dispute."

"So what can you do?"

"Me? I can protect her physically, give her emotional support, try to demystify the son of a bitch, until I can find a way to put him out of business."

"You're not afraid of him?" Tony said.

"No."

"How come?"

"It's what you get used to," I said. "My father was a cop. I was a cop. I know a lot of bad guys." I laughed a little. "Some of my husband's, former husband's, family are criminals."

"Really?"

"Not my husband," I said.

"It's hard to imagine you a policeman," Tony said.

"Because I'm so cute and perky?"

"Exactly," Tony said.

We both laughed.

"Melanie Joan says you're an artist," Tony said.

"I paint a little," I said.

"I'd love to see some of your work," Tony said.

"You'll have to come to Boston," I said. "I don't carry them with me."

"Maybe I will," Tony said.

Uh oh.

Tony nodded at the waitress and she brought us two fresh drinks. The bar was crowded but not noisy. He raised his glass toward me. I raised mine and we drank.

"So," he said. "You live alone in Boston?"

"I live with Rosie," I said.

"And Rosie is?"

"A miniature English bull terrier."

"And she's cute," Tony said.

"She's startlingly beautiful," I said.

"Like her mother," Tony said.

He was looking at me steadily. I knew where we were going, and I knew I had to decide if I wanted to go there. I took in a silent breath. Was I ready once again to take my clothes off in front of someone I didn't know terribly well? I took in another breath. At least my body was pretty good.

"Just like her mother," I said.

We were both quiet. He knew where we were going, too. And he knew I knew. We could feel it in the space around us.

"Are you someone who kisses on the first date?" Tony said.

"Depends on who the first date is with," I said.

"This first date is with me."

"I know," I said.

"And?"

"I might kiss on the first date."

"Is there somewhere that we can test the hypothesis?" Tony said.

I liked Tony.

"Melanie Joan and I have separate bedrooms," I said.

"And you think Melanie Joan will be in hers."

"I do."

"Wanna test the hypothesis?" Tony said.

"We'd be fools not to," I said.

The security guard in the corridor recognized me and nodded slightly as I unlocked the suite door. Melanie Joan had left the chain off. The living room was immaculate, and, on the small table in front of the window, there was a bottle of champagne in an ice bucket.

"Melanie Joan appears to have anticipated something," I said.

"Is it because she knows me?" Tony said. "Or because she knows you?"

"Maybe she's just an incurable romantic," I said.

"Like me," Tony said and put his arms around me and kissed me. I kissed him back. We moved to the couch. He began to fumble with my clothes. *Here we go!* I thought.

And I helped him with the buttons.

CHAPTER
THIRTY-THREE

We were going home from LA, a couple of good-looking babes, traveling first class, each with a Bloody Mary and a small foil envelope of smoked almonds. The plane bumped slightly. I tensed my knees. I wasn't actually afraid of flying, but I'd enjoy it more if I were driving.

"You and Tony seemed to hit it off very well," Melanie Joan said.

"We did."

"Every night," Melanie Joan said.

"How sweet of you to notice," I said.

Melanie Joan smiled. "Just envy," she said.

The cabin attendant passed out menus. Melanie Joan filed hers in the seat pocket.

"You're after Tony?" I said.

"Among others," Melanie Joan said. "My heels get rounder every year."

"Have you ever . . . ? I'm sorry, it's none of my business."

Melanie Joan shook her head. "Tony doesn't sleep with clients," she said.

"How very professional," I said.

The plane droned eastward. Lunch was served. I ate some of it. Melanie Joan knew better. She had a second Bloody Mary.

"You like him?" Melanie Joan said.

"Yes. I like him quite a lot."

"Will you stay in touch?" Melanie Joan said.

"Yes. I hope so."

Melanie Joan nodded and didn't say anything.

"What?" I said.

She shrugged.

"What?" I said again.

"Tony's very nice," Melanie Joan said. "But he's a Hollywood guy."

"Meaning?"

"You've been in six pitch meetings with me," Melanie Joan said. "All of the people in the meetings were Hollywood guys."

I nodded.

"Tony seems very genuine," I said.

Melanie Joan nodded.

"I'm in the business," I said, "of distinguishing genuine from pretend."

"I know."

"Even though we haven't been together for a terribly long time, we have been very intimately together in the time we've had."

Melanie Joan nodded.

"People reveal themselves," I said.

"During sex?"

"Yes."

"And you're happy with what he revealed?"

"Yes."

"Good," Melanie Joan said.

"I think he cares about me," I said.

"I'm sure he thinks so too," Melanie Joan said.

Maybe she really was jealous.

The cabin crew cleared the lunch, and offered us ice cream for dessert. Melanie Joan's superior travel skills became apparent. Melanie had some with chocolate sauce and butterscotch sauce and strawberries and whipped cream and nuts. I'd wasted too many calories on the entree and had to decline. Live and learn.

"Would you like a bite of my ice cream?" Melanie Joan said.

"No," I said grimly. "I would not."

CHAPTER
THIRTY-FOUR

The next morning Rosie woke me up at quarter to seven. It was only quarter to four on my still West Coast internal clock, and I wasn't pleased. But Rosie is very insistent in a charming way. By eight o'clock I had walked her and fed her and showered and put on my face. I was drinking coffee at my counter when Melanie Joan called me.

"He's here," she said.

"Here where?" I said.

"Outside my building. I can see him from my window."

"You should be all right," I said. "It's a secure building. Just stay inside until I get there."

She said she would. I hung up and called Spike. The morning traffic was still heavy and it was five past nine before we were able to come to Melanie Joan's rescue. There was no sign of John Melvin.

"He was right out there," Melanie Joan said, "standing on the corner of Dartmouth Street."

"Far enough away," I suspect, "so as not to violate the restraining order."

"That would be like him," Melanie Joan said.

Her shoulders were hunched in toward her chest. She rubbed her right forearm with her left hand as if the circulation were lagging. Her face was pinched as if she were cold.

"Goddamn him," she said.

Her voice was shaky.

"I thought in Los Angeles that I had some sort of breakthrough," she said. "That I was implacable in my resolve not to fear him."

"But you do," I said.

"Yes."

"Everyone fears things," I said.

Spike smiled. "Almost everyone," he said.

"Who's this?" Melanie Joan said.

"Spike," I said. "He's going to help us."

Melanie Joan didn't seem pleased about Spike but she made no comment until we were sitting in her living room with coffee.

"How is he going to help us?" she said.

"Hard to imagine, isn't it?" Spike said.

"I didn't mean it that way," Melanie Joan said.

Spike smiled at her.

"Here's what I've been thinking," I said. "I've been thinking that we can spend the rest of our lives guarding you against John Stalker. Or, we can put John Stalker out of business and solve the problem permanently."

Melanie Joan nodded. Spike drank some coffee and ate one of the miniature corn muffins Melanie Joan had presented on a silver salver.

"Is he going to, ah, put John out of business?" Melanie Joan said.

"No," I said. "I am. Spike is going to look out for you while I'm doing it."

"Look after me?"

"He won't stay here all the time," I said. "The building is secure. But when you need to go out, or if you're scared, Spike will be available to you."

"No."

"Spike is very formidable," I said. "He can keep you safe."

"I don't want a man hanging around me everywhere I go."

"Right on, sister," Spike said.

"See?" Melanie Joan said.

"Spike would joke at his own funeral," I said.

"I hope," Spike said.

I ignored him. "He can really take care of you," I said. "Better, probably, than I could."

She looked at Spike.

"And how long before the suggestive remarks begin?" Melanie Joan said.

Spike grinned.

"I am a practicing homosexual," he said.

She stared at him for a moment. "Homosexual?"

"Gayer than toe shoes," Spike said.

"My God," she said. "But you're so . . ."

"We don't all look like Michael Jackson," Spike said.

"Oh, no, of course not. I didn't mean . . . You're so large."

Spike smiled.

135

"The better to look after you, my dear," Spike said. He looked like a pleasant Kodiak bear.

"And what will you be doing," Melanie Joan said to me, "while Mr. Spike is here?"

"I can't believe this is the only thing John Melvin's ever done wrong," I said. "I'm going to see if I can find out what else he's done."

"And if you do?" Melanie Joan said.

"He can't stalk you if he's in jail."

"Oh my God," Melanie Joan said. "Can you send him to jail?"

"Let's find out," I said.

CHAPTER
THIRTY-FIVE

"If the therapy is effective," Max Copeland said, "his patients will share with Dr. Ex the fact of our interest."

"So if I go visit the women whose names I got through grueling surveillance, I'll give myself away."

"Probably," Copeland said. "One of the necessities of effective therapy is a trusting relationship between the therapist and the patient."

"Don't you think it a little odd," I said, "that in the first ten minutes of our first session, Dr. Ex was asking about my sexuality."

"Sexuality is an important question for a patient whose presenting symptoms include an inability to fully separate from a divorced spouse."

"Granted," I said. "But would you have asked right off the bat?"

"I might have let it emerge from the therapy," Copeland said. "But it would not be inappropriate to introduce the topic."

I said, "I know it's nothing I can prove, just a feeling . . ."

"This is not a court of law," Copeland said. "What you feel is probably more important in here than what you think."

"He's reacting to me sexually," I said.

Copeland nodded.

"I mean, I can feel it, any woman can feel it, if it's strong enough. It's like when he looks at me he's seeing me naked."

Copeland nodded again.

"It's not just me," I said. "I know the difference. You're not doing that."

Copeland smiled again and made a little motion with his head which indicated nothing more than that he'd heard me.

"I feel as if he's trying to penetrate me," I said.

"Well, in some sense, that is the business of therapy," Copeland said.

"It's not that," I said. "The man wants my soul."

Copeland tilted his head slightly and widened his eyes.

"Most men want to dominate you," I said. "Except Richie . . ."

"Your ex-husband," Copeland said.

"Yes. Richie was very non-controlling."

"Did you have any control over him?" Copeland asked.

I started to speak and stopped. I hadn't ever thought about controlling Richie.

"Well, I guess it depends on what you mean by control," I said. "We cared about each other, but we didn't *belong* to each other."

Copeland nodded and with his right hand made a tiny circular gesture that encouraged me to go on.

"We were a democracy," I said. "Not a kingdom."

"How did that make you feel?" Copeland said.

"Oh God," I said. "The ultimate therapy cliché. I knew it would come."

Copeland nodded. He didn't say anything. I was quiet too. I was not going to let him therapize these sessions. Copeland seemed perfectly comfortable with the silence. I could last as long as he could, the bastard. It was hard to sit motionless in the silence. I wanted to cross my legs, clear my throat, rub my hands together. I didn't. I sat still. I would outlast the bastard if it lasted the whole hour. The weight of the stillness pressed on my chest. I had trouble swallowing. All of a sudden there were tears in my eyes and on my face. I was, for crissake, crying. Copeland pushed a box of Kleenex closer to me on his desktop. The son of a bitch was prepared for everything. I wiped the tears on the Kleenex. My nose was running. I blew it on the Kleenex. Copeland moved a wastebasket nearer to me. I deposited the tissue.

"I don't know where this came from," I said.

My voice was shaky. I was still crying.

"Go ahead, let it come," Copeland said. "See what comes with it."

I shook my head. We sat some more until I got control.

"Well," I said. "I guess we know how it makes me feel."

My voice was still shaky. Copeland nodded. It was almost a nod of approval. Maybe.

CHAPTER
THIRTY-SIX

I sat at my kitchen counter that night and sipped white wine and talked on the phone for an hour and a half with Tony Gault.

"You've ruined my sex life," he said.

"I had hoped to enhance it," I said.

"Oh, God yes, you did. But now nobody else interests me."

"Not even the starlet of the week?"

"Especially not her."

"Is that because I'm so innovative in bed?"

"Yes. And also because I had forgotten the pleasure of boffing someone I could talk with after."

"Yes," I said. "I like that too."

"When are you coming back?" he said.

"I don't know. I'm still working for Melanie Joan, and . . . I need to stay on it for a while . . . Could you come east?"

"I'm working on it," Tony said. "But so far I can't contrive a reason."

"How about to see me?"

"I mean a business reason," Tony said. "Then I can get the agency to pick up the tab."

Rosie was lying in one of the armchairs near the coffee table by the window. She was curled up so that only one almond-shaped black eye was looking at me. But the gaze of that one eye was penetrating. I smiled at her and her tail thumped once against the arm of the chair.

"Do you miss me?" I said.

"Real bad," he said.

"Do you miss the lovely chats we had after?"

"Well," Tony said, "yes. But to tell you the truth I especially miss before the chats."

"So it's not just my mind?" I said.

"No," Tony said. "It's also your pelvis."

We talked awhile longer about pelvises until Tony said he had a client to meet for drinks at the Peninsula bar. We said goodbye and hung up. I felt like someone who had not drunk quite enough to quench her thirst.

I took my wineglass to the stove and sipped a little more while I cooked myself broccoli and pasta. When it was done I brought it to the window table and sat opposite Rosie to eat my supper. Rosie sat up briskly. Alert.

"Now here's the problem we have to resolve," I said to Rosie. "Should I talk to the people we spotted coming and going at his office? The several women, the two men. You remember?"

Rosie was looking at my pasta.

"If I do, they'll tell Melvin that some broad named Randall was asking about him."

I gave Rosie a small broccoli floret. She ate it as thoroughly as she did things she likes a lot better.

"Broccoli is good for you," I said. "He still won't know that Sunny Randall and Sonya Burke are the same."

I poured myself a little more wine.

"It might be good if he has a sense someone is after him. Stalking the stalker so to speak."

I giggled a little at my own cleverness. Talking to Rosie was perfectly normal. I did it all the time. Giggling at what I said to her was a sure sign that I had drunk too much. I looked at my wineglass. *So what?*

I took my wineglass with me to the kitchen counter and looked at my notebook.

"Okay," I said. "Tomorrow we'll start with Kim Crawford. Our lady of the silver Volvo."

I sat on the stool and leaned my back against my counter and looked at my reflection in the dark window across the room. Rosie had gone to sleep in the armchair. I raised my glass to my reflection. There I was, a woman in her middle thirties, living alone with a dog, getting drunk. Pathetic. Pretty soon I'd have to start listening to the tick of my biological clock. Tick tock. I wasn't even sure I wanted a baby. And if I did, who did I want to father it? Maybe Spike and I should have a child. We loved each other. We got along. He was funny and smart and brave . . . and gay!

I looked at myself some more.

"Hell," I said to Rosie. "I don't even own a turkey baster."

Richie was funny and smart and brave. We loved each other.

"And," I said, "I wouldn't need a turkey baster."

142

Wouldn't need one with Tony Gault, either. He was smart and funny. He might be brave. We had certainly gotten along in LA. When I thought about Tony, I thought about us together in bed. I thought about how strong he felt, and how supple. It was odd. I didn't think of him naked. I thought of myself naked in front of him. I felt it in the bottom of my stomach. It made my throat close a little. I wanted to be naked in front of him again.

". . . Could you come east?"

"I'm working on it. But so far I can't contrive a reason."

"How about to see me?"

"I mean a business reason. Then I can get the agency to pick up the tab."

Maybe I wasn't worth the airfare? Maybe being naked wasn't as important to Tony. But it was important to me. I wanted him here. I wanted him against me. I stood looking at myself. I looked good. I had a good body. Men liked it. I looked at Rosie sleeping in the armchair. I wondered why I had cried in Dr. Copeland's office.

CHAPTER
THIRTY-SEVEN

Kim Crawford lived in a condominium townhouse among a whole village of them off Route 2 in West Concord.

"My name is Sunny Randall," I said to her at the door. "I'm a detective and I need to talk with you."

"A detective?"

"Yes. It's not about you. It's just part of a thing I'm investigating."

"What?"

"Could I come in?"

"Oh, yes, sure," she said and held the door open. "Come on in. Don't mind the dog. You want some coffee or something?"

The dog I was asked not to mind appeared to be the Akita that ate Tokyo. He stood against her leg and looked at me the way big fighting dogs look at you. Not hostile exactly, more just appraising. I put my clenched fist down and let him sniff it. His tail wagged slightly. *Oh good.*

We sat in the living room. The townhouse looked as if it had been built on a tight budget. Everything looked thin. Except the Akita. Kim was barefoot, wearing jeans and a man's white tee shirt. She was carefully made up, and her blond hair was clean and slightly wavy. She had her feet tucked up on the sofa. Her toenails were painted.

I would have killed for that hair.

The Akita sat on the floor next to her and stared at me with his pale eyes.

"I can't tell you much about my investigation, Kim, it's confidential."

"I understand," Kim said.

The living room was done all in pink and gray. Over the mantel was a large framed color photograph of Kim in a wedding dress. The color had the garish tone that only wedding photos and class pictures can achieve. It did not go well with the rest of the room.

"Great picture," I said.

"Thanks. I love that dress."

I glanced around. There were no other pictures.

"And the groom?" I said.

"He dumped me a year and a half ago."

"Oh, I'm sorry," I said. "Any children?"

"No."

"So, you live here alone?"

"Me and Sam," she said and nodded at the dog. "Short for Samurai. He's a Japanese dog."

"I know," I said. "He's lovely."

"You got a dog?"

"Yes, I do, a bull terrier named Rosie."

"Dogs are great," Kim said. "You want some coffee? It's all made."

"Coffee would be nice," I said.

"I have Equal or sugar, and skim milk. I don't have any cream."

"Skim milk," I said, "would be perfect, and two little thingies of Equal."

"We're all the same, aren't we?" Kim said. "Worried sick about our figure, how we look. You married?"

"No," I said.

"So you're looking for a man too," Kim said.

I did one of those little noncommittal smile-nods I'd seen Copeland do.

"All the men I like are gay," Kim said. "All the straight men are jerks."

"It's hard to generalize," I said. "You're in therapy with Dr. Melvin?"

"Excuse me?"

"In the course of my investigation," I said, "I learned that you are a patient of Dr. John Melvin."

"So?"

"I don't wish to pry into your therapy, but could you tell me a bit about Dr. Melvin?"

"Why?"

"I'd rather leave it vague," I said. "Until we substantiate things."

"Are you investigating him?"

I did the smile-nod again. I was glad I'd discovered it.

"Has someone made a complaint or something?"

"Is there anything someone might complain about?" I said.

"Of course not. I just can't figure out why you're investigating him."

"Has he ever been, ah, inappropriate in your therapy?"

"Inappropriate?"

I nodded.

Kim didn't answer me. Her pretty, inexpressive face pinched a little around the mouth and at the corners of her eyes.

"Do you and he talk about your divorce?" I said.

"Of course. That's why I went to see him."

"And he's helped?"

"Oh yes, he's helped me a lot."

"Anything you don't like about him?" I said.

"Of course not. He's an absolutely wonderful man."

"Is he expensive?" I said.

"Paying the cost is part of the commitment," Kim said.

"I've heard that," I said. "Does your health insurance cover it?"

Kim shook her head.

"Do you earn a lot of money?" I said.

I glanced around the room as if it were obviously expensive.

"Alimony," she said.

"Dr. Melvin, too?"

Kim's face was suddenly infused with energy.

"The son of a bitch didn't get out of it cheap," Kim said.

I smiled. "I wish I'd had your divorce lawyer," I said.

It was a lie. I didn't want Richie to send me money. Though he did sometimes, because he felt like it. *You shared the hard times*, he would say. *You might as well share the good*. It was a myth that Richie liked to perpetuate. There had been bad emotional times. But there was always money.

"I hope it kills him every month to send that check."

I nodded. "What's your ex's name?" I said.

"Kerry Crawford, the bastard. It used to be Kim and Kerry, you know. It sounded good."

"It does sound good," I said. "Do you know a man named Dirk Beals?"

Again the vacant little face got pinched at the corners.

"Who's he?"

"Drives a black Porsche Boxster."

"Never heard of him," Kim said.

She put her hand on the Akita's massive head and patted him slowly. She probably wasn't aware she did it. The Akita had no reaction. He sat in his large containment and looked at me with his pale expressionless eyes.

If I weren't a heroic girl detective, I might have been a little afraid of him.

"Can I get you any more coffee?" Kim said.

What she meant was *It's time for you to go now. I don't want to talk with you anymore.*

"No," I said. "Thanks, I've got to run."

I reached over carefully and scratched the Akita behind his right ear. I don't know if he liked it. He permitted it.

"Dr. Melvin isn't in some kind of trouble, is he?"

"What kind could he be in?" I said.

148

"He couldn't be in any kind, unless some patient is lying about him."

"What kind of lies might they tell?" I said.

"I don't know. There isn't anything. I mean he's a fabulous shrink."

"I'm sure he is," I said. "Do you see him regularly?"

"Twice a week," Kim said. "Mondays and Thursdays."

"Mornings?" I said.

"Evenings, actually."

"I didn't think he had office hours in the evening," I said.

Her faced pinched again. "Dr. Melvin makes time for me in the evening," Kim said. "It's more convenient."

"That's good of him," I said.

"Yes."

"What does your ex-husband do that he can pay you all this alimony?" I said.

"He's a real estate broker," Kim said.

"In Concord?"

Kim shook her head. "Arlington," she said.

"Well, it's good he can afford it," I said.

"He'd better," Kim said.

Kerry Crawford, Arlington.

CHAPTER
THIRTY-EIGHT

Sonya Burke crossed her legs in the straight armchair across from Dr. Melvin, aware that she was showing a lot of leg.

"He dumped me a year and a half ago," I said.

Dr. Melvin wore a beautiful black suit with a white shirt. The shirt had a Windsor collar and French cuffs. His cuff links were black onyx with a small diamond chip in the center. He nodded gently.

"But he's paying for it," I said.

He raised his eyebrows.

"Alimony," I said.

"Ah," he said and smiled a little. "Does that make you feel less angry toward him?"

"I'm not angry toward him," I said. "But if he's going to dump me he's going to pay for the privilege."

Melvin nodded.

"Besides." I tried a grim smile. "It supports me while I look for another man."

Melvin nodded.

"It seems that all the men I like are gay. The straight men are jerks."

"And you need straight men," Melvin said.

"Of course."

"Because you need sex."

"Sure."

"More than occasional sex with Richie?" Melvin said.

"Yes."

"You're an attractive woman," Melvin said. "That should not be an issue."

"I don't want to sleep with jerks," I said.

"Who do you want to sleep with?"

I felt a tiny thrill in the center of my stomach. *The bait was out there, floating on the surface.*

"Men with brains," I said, "and maybe a little style, some authority."

"Talk about that a little more."

"I like men I can respect," I said.

"What do you respect?"

"I like men I can look up to. It's probably what drew me to Richie."

"What did you admire in him?" Melvin said.

He was perfectly still, watching me closely, his legs crossed at the ankle, leaning back in his chair, his hands folded over his stomach. I thought a minute.

"He was, he is, so in control of himself and his own life."

Melvin nodded. His big dark eyes stayed steady on me. He raised his eyebrows.

"I loved that in him," I said.

Melvin waited.

"But, with us," I said, "he wouldn't take control."

"Did you?"

"Take control? No. I couldn't. I didn't want it. I wanted him to give us direction. He'd always say, "whatever you'd like." For Christ's sake, I wanted to like what he liked."

I thought I was chumming the water. But I had the uneasy sense that what had begun as a story to trap him had slithered awfully close to a therapeutic admission.

"Have there been other men in your life like that?" Melvin said.

"My father . . ." *My father? Where the hell am I going?* "My father probably made every decision my mother was ever involved in."

"And with you?"

"He always supported anything I wanted to do."

"But he didn't tell you what that should be?"

"No."

"Like Richie."

"My God," I said. "Am I a living breathing cliché? Do I suffer from Oedipal conflict?"

Melvin smiled.

"Parents often have a great influence on us when we're children," he said. "And the influences sometimes linger."

"Oh, God," I said. "That's such a shrinky thing to say."

Melvin smiled at me. His voice was kind and almost amused.

"Miss Burke," he said. "I am a shrink."

I almost liked him at that moment.

"My mother was always bossy and mouthy," I said. "And if you listened to her you'd think she was completely in charge of everything."

"But she wasn't," Melvin said.

"No. In fact she was scared of nearly everything and really wasn't very good at anything and needed him to, you know, take complete care of her."

"And of you?"

"Yes. I was always uneasy when he was at work. I felt as if he were the adult, and I had been left alone with another kid."

"He was a very powerful man."

I nodded.

"And you want to be with someone like him?"

"I guess," I said.

"And do you want to be like your mother?"

"God, no," I said.

Melvin smiled slightly and sat back. All his motions were minimal, but the force of our interaction made them larger than they were. I waited. He didn't say anything. I didn't know what to say so I waited.

Finally, he said, "So you'd like to have a husband like your father, but you don't want to be a wife like your mother."

"Sort of a rock and a hard place," I said.

He nodded.

CHAPTER
THIRTY-NINE

I took Rosie for her morning stroll up Summer Street to the bridge, and back, and when I got to my building a man got out of a Porsche Boxster and spoke to me.

"Sunny Randall?" he said.

"Yes."

"My name is Dirk Beals. I wonder if we might talk."

He was slender and dark and much taller than I was. His hair had receded enough to qualify for Rogaine. He had on small round wire-rimmed glasses, and a very expensive gray tweed jacket. A long black wool scarf was wrapped around his neck a couple of times, with the loose end draped over his left shoulder.

"Sure," I said.

"Perhaps we could talk in your office?"

He paid no attention to Rosie, who was sniffing his ankles. I had made the bed before we went out for our walk. There was no lingerie laying around.

"Certainly," I said. "Home, studio, and office."

We went up in what used to be the freight elevator without speaking, and got off at my floor and went into my loft. I let Rosie off the leash and she went to her water dish. The loft looked great. The sun flooded in through the skylight and gleamed through the high industrial windows along my front wall. Beals looked around quite carefully, but he made no comment. I had turned on my coffeemaker before Rosie and I had gone for our walk, and the smell of fresh coffee perfumed the place.

"I'm having coffee," I said. "Would you care for some?"

"No."

I gestured at one of the armchairs in the window bay, and went to my counter and put coffee, milk, and sugar in a stainless-steel mug. Beals didn't sit. He stood where he was and continued to look around the room. I sat on a stool and swung around so my back was against the counter.

"What can I do for you," I said.

"You only have one room?" he said.

"But it's a very big one," I said.

Rosie finished drinking and looked at Beals for a moment and then went down the length of the loft and jumped up onto my bed and lay down and looked up with her head resting on her front paws.

"You live here alone?"

"Of course not," I said. "I live here with Rosie."

"Where is she?"

"The dog," I said.

He looked as if the answer annoyed him. He had a petulant self-satisfied face that looked like almost anything might annoy him.

"What can I do for you," I said.

"I'm an attorney," he said.

"That's not my fault," I said.

155

He was not amused.

"I understand you've been talking to Kimberly Crawford."

"Oh?"

"Ms. Crawford's emotional stability is precarious," Beals said. "Harassment will endanger it."

"I'm sure it will," I said, "if anyone ever harasses her."

"Don't be cute, missy," Beals said.

Missy?

"My sister is cute too," I said.

"I warn you right now," Beals said, "you are not to talk to or see Ms. Crawford again."

"Is she your client?" I said.

"She is the patient of my client."

"So you represent John Melvin," I said.

It rocked him a little. He started to speak and stopped and considered for a moment.

"Who I represent does not concern you," he said.

"But you know Kim Crawford," I said.

"That doesn't concern you either."

"Isn't it odd for a shrink's lawyer to know a shrink's patients?"

His face got red, and I watched, sort of fascinated, as the redness spread up over his forehead and darkened where he was bald.

After a moment, he said, "I don't believe you quite understand what you are dealing with here."

"I do," I said. "I'm dealing with a pompous jerk. But it's okay. I'm used to it."

"You are putting yourself in a dangerous position, missy."

He said it again!

"Why?"

"Because you are involved in something you don't understand. With powerful men that can make things happen." He paused for effect. "Bad things, if necessary."

"What am I involved with?" I said.

He looked at me without speaking. He must have really needed the glasses. The lenses were so thick they distorted his eyes.

"What am I involved with?" I said.

He stepped closer to me. He was breathing audibly. And something was twitching along his right cheekbone.

"You are involved, bitch, with floating facedown and naked in the Charles River."

His face was slightly moist. I put my cup down and stood.

"Hold on a minute," I said. "I want to show you something."

He didn't answer. I walked past him and behind my kitchen counter and opened the broom closet and took out a double-barreled ten-gauge sawed-off shotgun that my father had once taken from a drug dealer, and given to me, illegally, when I went into business for myself. I brought the weapon up to my shoulder and squinted at his face along the barrel. His eyes widened.

"You," I said, "are involved in me blowing your goddamned head off."

"Don't point that at me," he said.

"Why don't you and Melvin want me talking with Kim Crawford?" I said.

He shook his head. I kept the shotgun pointed at his face.

"Don't," he said.

Then he turned suddenly and ran from my loft. I let him go. When he was gone, I locked my door and put the shotgun on the counter and breathed quietly for a while until my heart stopped pounding.

CHAPTER
FORTY

When I went to see Melanie Joan, I brought Rosie. I didn't want to leave her alone. There had been something quite disturbing in Dirk Beals's damp preppy menace. When we came into Melanie Joan's apartment, Spike was on the couch with his feet on the coffee table, reading *Ring* magazine.

"Are you absolutely sure you're gay?" I said to him.

"Don't tell the guys at the Design Center," Spike said.

Rosie jumped up on the couch and lapped Spike's face. Melanie Joan came out of the room she wrote in.

"He cooks," Melanie Joan said to me. "He cleans up. It's like having a large maid."

Spike finally got Rosie to stop lapping him and she settled down on the couch next to him. Melanie Joan and I sat in facing armchairs on either side of the picture window that looked out over Copley Square.

"Everything been all right?" I said.

"Yes," she said. "He hasn't made an appearance."

I felt a little jab of disappointment. I had half hoped that Melvin would have given Spike a chance at him. I couldn't ask Spike to intervene, but if it was beyond my control . . . Oh well.

"What do you hear from your agent?" I said.

"Tony?"

"Yes."

"No one has gotten back to us on the pitches," Melanie Joan said.

We were silent, looking out the window. The Copley Plaza Hotel, built in the days of grand hotels, and still stately, was diagonally across from us.

"He call you?" Melanie Joan said.

I shook my head.

"Not for a while," I said.

We looked at the Copley Plaza some more.

"You have to remember," Melanie Joan said. "Tony is a Hollywood guy."

"Which makes him automatically insincere?" I said.

Without looking up from his magazine, Spike said, "You can fit all the sincerity in Hollywood on the head of a pin with enough room left over for three caraway seeds and an agent's heart."

We both stared at him.

"Did you just make that up?" I said.

"No," Spike said. "Fred Allen made it up."

"Fred Allen?" Melanie Joan said.

"Spike is a show business person," I said. "Do you know a man named Dirk Beals?"

Melanie Joan's face didn't pinch at the corners, like Kim Crawford's had. But it got more angular.

"I know him," she said.

I waited. She didn't say anything. Out of the corner of my eye I saw Spike look up from his magazine.

"Tell me about him," I said.

160

"Why do you ask?"

"His name came up in the investigation," I said.

Melanie Joan nodded.

"Can you tell me about him?" I said.

"Only if I must."

"He came to my loft this morning and threatened me," I said.

Spike dog-eared his magazine and sat up.

"My God," Melanie Joan said. "Was it about me?"

"I don't know," I said. "I had talked with one of your . . . with one of John Melvin's patients. The next day Beals comes around and tells me not to talk with her again."

"What did you do?" Melanie Joan said.

"I pointed a shotgun at him and told him I might blow his head off."

On the couch, Spike smiled.

Melanie Joan said, "Oh . . . my . . . God."

I waited. Everything had become corners and planes in Melanie Joan's face.

"What can you tell me?" I said.

"He is a repulsive human being," Melanie Joan said.

I nodded.

"He tried . . ." She paused and looked at Spike.

"You want me to step out?" Spike said.

Melanie Joan thought about it.

"No," she said. "There's nothing shameful about it. I need to get over that."

Spike shrugged and stayed where he was. I was quiet. Melanie Joan stared out the window.

Without looking at me, she said, "He tried to rape me."

"How dreadful," I said.

"It was more dreadful than you think," Melanie Joan said.

"Did he hurt you?" I said.

"No. My husband was present."

"Present?"

"He was watching."

Spike put his hand on Rosie's neck and let it rest there.

"Watching?" I said.

"It apparently excited him," Melanie Joan said.

Her voice was tinny.

"Good God!" I said.

"I kneed him," Melanie Joan said, "and pulled loose and ran out of the house."

"The house in Chestnut Hill?"

"Yes. I never went back."

"That's how you left your husband?" I said.

"Yes."

The room was silent except for the sound of Rosie snoring faintly against Spike's leg.

"Have you seen a shrink?" I said.

"I've had quite enough," Melanie Joan said in her flat tin voice, "of psychiatrists, thank you."

We were very quiet. Even Spike didn't know what to say.

Finally I said, "I am going to put them both away where they cannot bother you."

Melanie Joan's face was expressionless.

162

"Then you might as well put the other one away, too," she said.

Her voice was barely audible.

"Other one?" I said.

"Barry," she said. "Barry Clay. He was there. I think it was going to be his turn next."

"Are they both friends of Melvin's?" I said.

"Yes." She made a sound that might have been a humorless laugh. "The three musketeers."

"The other guy," I said.

"Other guy?"

"I saw Beals and another man leave Melvin's home late one night, and drive off in Beals's car."

"That was probably Barry," Melanie Joan said.

I looked at Spike. He looked as close to shocked as Spike could probably get.

"These are some sick heterosexuals," Spike said.

I nodded.

"Maybe you ought to bring Richie into this," Spike said.

"And Uncle Felix?"

"Felix would solve your problems the same day you called . . . and Melanie Joan's."

"I can't do that," I said.

"I could call for you," Spike said.

"That's not the point and you know it."

"Just a thought," Spike said.

"I can't be a grown-up detective and call my ex-husband every time I run into meanies."

Spike shrugged. He wasn't much for abstractions.

"I could call on them," Spike said.

"I have to deal with this, Spike."

Melanie Joan said, "What is he talking about? Who is this Felix?"

"My husband's uncle," I said.

"And what could he do?"

"He'd kill them," I said.

Melanie Joan didn't say anything for a moment, then she looked at Spike.

"And you," she said. "Would you kill them too?"

"Probably not," Spike said. "But I'd get their attention."

"How?"

Spike smiled. "I don't go into things with any preconceptions," Spike said. "I'd ask them not to bother you or Sunny, and I'd see what developed."

"These are very dangerous people," Melanie Joan said.

Spike smiled. Melanie Joan looked at me.

"They are very dangerous, Sunny."

"I'll be careful," I said. "You'll be safe with Spike."

"I thought gay men were supposed to be, sort of, you know, sissies," Melanie Joan said.

"Sometimes I scratch and bite," Spike said.

"Maybe you could talk with Uncle Whatsisname," Melanie Joan said.

"Felix," I said. "You want me to have them killed?"

Melanie Joan looked out the window for a moment at the spot across Huntington Avenue where John Melvin had been standing. Then she looked slowly back at me.

"Yes," she said. "I would like that very much."

CHAPTER
FORTY-ONE

Kerry Crawford had an office on Massachusetts Avenue in Arlington, across the street from a restaurant called Flora, where Julie and I went to dinner sometimes. He had wavy black hair and a great tan. There were four desks in the office plus a little alcove in the back where Kerry sat at a slightly bigger desk. There were photographs of houses in the front window, and all over the walls inside. Two of the desks were empty. A sturdy woman with bluish hair and sensible shoes sat at the other one talking on the phone.

"You're investigating my ex-wife?" he said.

He had a voice like a television announcer, with no hint of region to it.

"Not really," I said. "She's peripheral to a case I'm working on."

"So what did she do?"

"Does she often *do* things?"

"She's wacky," Crawford said. "Hell, I even sent her to a shrink toward the end."

"Because?"

"She was so freaking clingy. It was driving me crazy. 'I love you do you love me?' You know? All the time, for crie eye."

"Did that help her?" I said.

Crawford pursed his lips, trying to think how to say it.

"It sort of ended our sex life," he said after a time.

"Do you know why?"

He shrugged.

"No. All of a sudden she didn't want to very often, and even when she'd let me she'd lie there stiff, and not move, you know, like close your eyes and think of England?"

"Did you ever talk about it?" I said.

"I raised hell about it. But it didn't do any good."

"How odd," I said.

"Yeah. For crissake she wouldn't even say anything about it. Just froze up on me."

"Is that why you left her?"

He nodded.

"I guess so," he said. "She used to be hot, always wanted it."

"She still tell you she loved you?" I said.

"Yeah." Crawford shook his head. "God," he said. "I can't figure women out."

"Was she always asking if you loved her too?"

Crawford looked surprised. "Yeah," he said. "I used to say to her, 'I married you didn't I? And I support you, and I bop you whenever you want.' "

"And that didn't reassure her?" I said.

"Not for long," Crawford said. "But she'd keep saying she loved me."

"That must have been frustrating," I said.

"You better believe it," Crawford said. "I'd say to her, 'If you love me so goddamned much how come you don't come across anymore?' You know?"

I nodded. "And she froze up after she started seeing this psychiatrist?"

"Yeah."

"What was his name?"

"Melvin, Dr. Melvin," Crawford said. "Supposed to be some kind of specialist. I think he's a fucking quack. Excuse my French."

"*Certainement*," I said. "Did the freeze come right away?"

"No. It was after she'd been seeing him awhile, maybe two, three months."

"And she never said why?"

"No. So what the hell was I supposed to do? I don't get it at home, I get it someplace else."

"Anyone would," I said.

"You married?"

"No."

"Good," he said. "Maybe we could get together for something interesting."

"I thought you had remarried."

"So?"

"So we probably won't get together."

"Hey, Sunny." He gave me a big lounge-lizard smile. "My wife's married; I'm not."

I stood. And gave him a business card.

"If you think of anything else about Dr. Melvin or Kim, please give me a call," I said.

"Even if I don't think of anything," Crawford said.

I would just as soon have dated a rabid hyena, but I didn't want to shut him off. I might need to talk with him again.

"Sure," I said.

CHAPTER
FORTY-TWO

I was having juice and coffee at my counter, opening the mail. There was a big manila envelope. I opened it. Inside was a color Xerox print of a naked woman lying on a couch. Someone had pasted on a grainy picture of my head, with a knit cap pulled down around my ears. *I must remember not to wear that hat anymore, pulled down over my ears it makes me look like my mother*. I took the picture to the window and looked at it in the daylight. It was obviously a blowup of a picture taken of me outside. I had bought the hat only three weeks ago, so the picture was recent. There was nothing to identify the woman or the room. I looked at Rosie.

"Her body isn't so great," I said.

She sat on her tail and dropped her jaw and put her ears back and looked more like a bull terrier than I had thought it possible for a bull terrier to look. I looked at the picture again. Then I called Brian Kelly.

"I have a picture," I said. "Via the U.S. Postal Service."

"And it arrived?" Brian said. "Intact?"

"If I drop it off, could you get it processed through forensics?"

"Sooner or later," Brian said.

169

"They're still promising things by the twelfth of never?" I said.

"Busy busy," Brian said. "You trying to establish the origin?"

"I know the origin. I'm trying to get proof."

"Do what I can," Brian said.

"The picture is of a nude woman."

"Excellent," Brian said.

"Someone has pasted my face onto her body."

"Your story," Brian said.

"It's not me," I said.

"I'll be able to tell," Brian said.

"My God," I said. "I think I'm blushing."

Brian laughed a little bit. "Do you know why the picture was sent?"

"To discourage me from an investigation," I said.

"Are there threats included?"

"Implied," I said.

"Same thing we spoke of before?"

"Yes."

"Do you need a hand with the threat part, maybe?"

"No," I said. "I'm doing fine with it."

"Okay," he said. "Let me know if you change your mind."

"I will," I said. "But I won't."

"Sure," Brian said. "Bring it by. I'll find out when I can, as fast as I can get the lab to do it."

When I hung up, I finished breakfast and took a shower and put on my face, and got dressed. I took my gun, and said goodbye to Rosie. I went out to my car. I looked around the street. I didn't see anything. I looked back at my building for a minute.

"I think I won't leave Rosie alone," I said out loud. And went back in and got her and took her with me.

She was very pleased.

CHAPTER
FORTY-THREE

I wore my gun behind my right hipbone on a wide black belt with a nice silver buckle. It was more accessible than it was in my purse, and quick access might be a good thing, following Dirk Beals around. Beals had a townhouse on the flat of Mt. Vernon Street, near Brimmer Street. At 8a.m. I was parked beside a hydrant a half block up toward Charles Street, drinking coffee. It was early for Rosie. She was asleep on the passenger seat. At 8:10 a traffic warden stopped by the car and waved at me to move. I held up my badge and she nodded and moved on. The badge said BAIL ENFORCEMENT AGENT in lettering around the edge, and there was a big blue seal with an eagle on it in the center. I had bought the badge on the Internet. Few people actually look at badges.

At 8:35 a brown and white Boston cab pulled up in front of Beals's townhouse, and the man himself came out wearing a Burberry trench coat and carrying a briefcase on a shoulder strap. I followed the cab down Storrow Drive and up Cambridge Street, down New Street past District 1 Station and on into the financial district. Beals got out and went into 53 State. I left my car by another hydrant, brought Rosie with me on her leash in case they towed the car, went in, and looked at the lobby directory. He was there, Dirk Beals Ltd. on the thirtieth floor. We went back to the car, which had not been towed. Rosie got in the backseat and looked at pedestrians. I used the car phone to call information and get the number and call Beals Ltd. A woman answered.

"Dirk Beals," she said.

"Hi," I said, "it's Jenny from the Better Business Control Office. What business do you do?"

"Financial management," she said. "Who did you say you were?"

"Thank you very much," I said.

I followed Beals all that day, and the next two, and the fact that he had a financial management company at 53 State Street was the sum of what I learned. He went to work in the morning. He ate lunch with different people every day. He went home at night. For a fiend he lived a boring life.

On the fourth morning I decided to give it one more day, before I tried something else. And it turned out well for me. Beals did the same old thing: work in the morning, lunch with someone at noon, except this time the lunch was with the guy that had been with him outside Melvin's office. They strolled down to the Meridien Hotel. I left my dog and car with the doorman, and followed Beals and his friend up the escalator at a discreet distance. They took a table in Cafe Fleuri, and I went back downstairs and lingered obscurely in the lobby until they came down. When they came out I stayed with them on foot. When they reached 53 State, Beals went in and his friend kept walking. I stayed with the friend. He walked on down through Quincy Market to the parking garage. When he went in, I waited outside, and in a few minutes he drove out in a black Saab sedan and drove away. I got the license number. Then I walked back to the Meridien, duked the doorman a twenty, and got in my car.

"I gave Rosie a little walk," the doorman said. "She did a nice doody."

As we drove away I smiled at Rosie, who was sitting in the passenger seat again, looking back toward the doorman.

"You make friends everywhere," I said.

CHAPTER
FORTY-FOUR

I called Tony Gault at one minute past noon, my time.
His secretary said he was in a meeting.

"May he call you back," the secretary said.

"Yes," I said and hung up.

One minute past nine his time and he's already in a
meeting. It had not occurred to me until now that I
didn't have his home phone number. Why didn't I?

It was Richie's turn to have Rosie, and he showed
up, on time, he was annoyingly punctual, at one
o'clock. Rosie ran around and chased her tail and
jumped on and off the furniture and wiggled. Which
was also a little annoying.

"You want some coffee?" I said.

"Sure," Richie said.

He sat in a chair in my window alcove with Rosie in
his lap, a compact muscular man, with thick black hair
cut short. There was a stillness in Richie that I had
never really understood. He never seemed uncomfortable with quiet. He'd be a good match for Dr.
Copeland. They'd probably sit and look calmly at each
other for the full fifty minutes. I put his coffee down in
front of him and took mine and sat in the armchair
across from him.

"So how's everything with Ms. Right," I said.

"Carrie and I are fine," Richie said.

"What's Carrie's last name?"

"LeClair," Richie said.

"Carrie LeClair," I said. "Cute name."

Richie nodded.

"I've been seeing a shrink," I said.

"Un huh."

"Part of a case," I said. "I'm not getting therapy."

Richie smiled.

"We did that," he said.

"You know who Dr. Melvin is," I said.

"Melanie Joan's ex."

"And you know I'm seeing him, undercover, sort of, to see if I can get some leverage on him."

"You've rejected this before, but my uncle Felix could leverage him right out of the picture if you'd like."

"You know I can't do that," I said.

Richie nodded.

"So, I'm seeing another shrink," I said. "Dr. Copeland, to help me understand the other shrink."

"Good shrink, bad shrink," Richie said.

"Exactly," I said, "and the ploy with the bad shrink is to tell him as much truth about my problems as I can so it'll ring true."

Richie drank some coffee.

"And the good shrink asked me about us, and I said we were a democracy, not a kingdom. And he asked me how that made me feel and I cried."

Richie looked at me over the half-raised coffee cup.

176

"That sounds suspiciously like therapy," Richie said.

"I know. He keeps doing that to me."

"Why did you cry?"

"I don't know."

"Does the good shrink have any thoughts?"

"We haven't talked about it," I said. "But it came up in Dr. Melvin's office and he suggested that I wanted you to be like my father, but I didn't want to be like my mother."

"You sure he hasn't penetrated your disguise?" Richie said.

Rosie sniffed at Richie's coffee and snapped her head away. Hot.

"What do you think?" I said.

"About why you cried?"

"Yes."

"What did you mean about it not being a kingdom," Richie said.

"I meant you weren't in charge," I said. "That we shared responsibility equally."

"And then you cried?"

"Yes."

"I assume you were crying because I wasn't in charge and we shared responsibility equally."

"That's ridiculous. Why would I cry about that?"

"I'm not licensed in this area," Richie said. "I just figure you say something, then you cry, it's probably what you said that's making you cry."

"You think I didn't want responsibility?"

"I don't know."

"What do you think, I want to be like my mother?"

"I wouldn't think so," Richie said.

"I'm not like my mother," I said.

"I know," Richie said. "I never thought I was like your father."

"You weren't," I said.

I felt my eyes begin to fill up.

"Goddamn it," I said. "Goddamn it."

"I didn't mean to make you cry," Richie said.

I nodded.

"You asked," Richie said.

"I know," I said. "I know I fucking asked."

Richie put his coffee cup down and carefully put Rosie on the floor and stood.

"I think Rosie and I will be going now," he said.

I was dabbing at my eyes with a paper napkin. Richie got Rosie's leash from the hook on the back of the door and put it on. Rosie jumped around with excitement. She was going out.

"I'm sorry you feel bad," Richie said.

"Don't let that goddamned Carrie LeCluck order my dog around," I said.

"LeClair," Richie said. "She doesn't order Rosie."

My voice was too shaky. I shook my head.

"Call me if you need to," Richie said.

I was struggling not to cry a loud "boo hoo" cry. I shook my head again.

"Or not," Richie said and left with Rosie.

CHAPTER
FORTY-FIVE

When Rosie was gone I missed her. I also usually had a nag of guilty pleasure that I was for a short time responsible for no one but myself. This time I wasn't so sure being entirely alone with myself was something I wanted. It gave me time to think. And thinking led me to wondering about myself and my life and the history of my marriage and whether there might be something wrong with me. Was I unable to love anyone enough to keep them?

To be doing something, I called Brian Kelly. He said the black Saab driven by Dirk Beals's friend was registered to Barry Clay, M.D., with an address in the Back Bay. He also said the lab had not yet processed the pictures, but that he had studied the nude one.

"Am I invited to the wedding?" I said.

"Of course, unless you plan to talk a lot about our sex life."

"Yours and mine? Only to the bride."

"Well, at least speak well of it."

"It's been so long, I forgot," I said.

"You were thrilled," Brian said.

We hung up and I added Barry Clay's name to my list. I wasn't really quite sure what it was a list of.

Possibilities, maybe. I put the list away and got another cup of coffee and took it with me to my easel. I worked for a while on the Weeks Footbridge painting. I wanted very much to get the sense of arching tranquillity that I always saw when I looked at the bridge live. I tried changing the perspective of the river's edge looking below the bridge toward Cambridge.

Ever since the marriage had stopped working, I had tried to figure out what was wrong with Richie. Now I was forced, even when I was keeping busy, during momentary lapses when I couldn't avoid it, to wonder what, perhaps, was wrong with me. It was unpleasant to think about. It interfered with my concentration.

At ten o'clock Los Angeles time I put my brushes away and called Tony Gault again. He had just stepped out of the office. She'd give him my message as soon as he came back. I hung up and walked the bright length of my loft a couple of times. It was perfectly silent. I was the only life in the place.

The phone rang. I started to pick it up, stopped myself, and held back until it had rung twice more.

I picked it up and said hello. It was Spike.

"I took Melanie Joan over to the David Brudnoy show last night. Melvin was watching us from across the street."

"Did you do anything?"

"I started across the street but Melanie Joan screamed at me not to leave her alone, and Melvin got in somebody's car and they drove off."

"What car?"

180

"Black Saab sedan, Mass plates," Spike said. He gave me the plate numbers.

"Barry Clay," I said.

"You know already," Spike said.

"I'm a detective."

"Probably the world's cutest," Spike said.

"If I'm so fucking cute," I said, "why can't I hang onto a man?"

"You're hanging onto me," Spike said.

"I was thinking more of the heterosexual persuasion."

"You can't have everything," Spike said.

"Well, okay, will you marry me?" I said.

"God, no," Spike said. "But I'll be your walker, if you'd like."

"That's so sweet," I said. "What was your plan if Melanie Joan hadn't screamed at you, and Melvin hadn't driven away."

"I was going to clean his clock," Spike said.

"No," I said.

"No?"

"If you, as her agent, assault somebody," I said, "it makes Melanie Joan liable. Dr. Melvin is just the sort of creepy crawly that would sue her."

"But I can assault someone to protect her," Spike said.

"Absolutely," I said. "But only that."

"Well," Spike said, "you certainly aren't any fun."

"I know," I said.

We hung up. I got out my phone book and looked up Barry Clay, M.D. He was an allergist with offices in

Brookline. So what? I looked at my list of possibilities again. I could go see the woman who drove the car registered to Augustus J. Walsh, or the woman driving the Acura, who lived in Groveland, and whose name was Sally Millwood. Or I could hang around the empty loft and think about what was wrong with me. I decided I'd rather drive to Winchester than Groveland, so I put my gun in my purse and went.

CHAPTER
FORTY-SIX

No one was home at the Augustus J. Walsh home, which was on a small cul-de-sac called Raleigh Terrace, off of Route 3. A neighbor told me they were in Florida for the winter but she didn't know where. So it was Groveland after all.

The town is located west of Newburyport and south of Haverhill, and fifteen miles from nowhere. I got directions at Jerry's Convenience store in downtown Groveland. Actually, Jerry's Convenience appeared to be downtown Groveland.

Sally Millwood's house was small and gray-shingled. There was no garage. The driveway was two-wheel ruts in the lawn, and the Acura I'd seen at Dr. Melvin's was parked there. Parked behind it was a black Ford pickup.

A young man in work boots, blue jeans, and a white tee shirt opened the door for me. He had *Semper Fi* tattooed in blue script on his left forearm, and his long hair was pulled back into a ponytail. The hair was held in place by a twisted rubber band. He stared at me without speaking.

"Is Sally Millwood here?" I said.

He stared at me for another long moment.

"Sally's dead."

"Oh, I'm terribly sorry. Are you Mr. Millwood?"

He shook his head.

"Robert Benedetto," he said. "We lived here together."

"Mr. Benedetto, I'm sorry, but can you talk with me for a minute?"

"About what?"

"I'm a detective," I said. "I need to know a little about Sally's death."

He looked at me some more. There was no expression in his eyes. Then he stepped out of the house and closed the door.

"House is a mess," he said. "Whaddya want to know."

"How did she die?" I said.

"Drug overdose, they said."

"Who said?"

"Ambulance people."

"Was there an autopsy?"

"I don't think so."

"Who found her?"

He paused, took a packet of Marlboros out of his back pocket, lit one, and put the pack away. Without taking the cigarette from his mouth, he inhaled a lot of smoke and let it out.

"I did," he said.

"And you called?"

"Cops."

"Tell me about it."

"Cops came and took a look at her and right away called the ambulance. Ambulance guys said she had no pulse and it looked like she'd OD'd."

"Did they take her to a hospital?"

"Haverhill," he said. "Mary Murphy."

"Did she use drugs?"

He shook his head.

"None?"

He shook his head again, squinting a little as the cigarette smoke drifted up past his eyes.

"So how do you explain the overdose."

"She didn't have no overdose," he said.

"Then what did she die of?"

He took the cigarette out of his mouth and flicked the ashes off it, and put it back in his mouth and took a long drag on it. The smoke came out with his words.

"I don't know. I just know she never used no drugs. I was thinking maybe it might be like one of those kids they find dead in bed."

"Sudden Infant Death Syndrome," I said.

"Yeah, that. I figure maybe it can happen to grown-ups."

"Did you tell people this?"

"I ain't her husband. They don't want to hear me. I said they should cut her open, find out what killed her. But her old lady said no. Nobody's gonna cut up her baby. So they said it was a drug OD and buried her."

"Did she see a doctor at the hospital?"

"Figueredo," Benedetto said. "Puerto Rican guy. Dr. Figueredo."

All of this was recited to me like someone doing rote memory exercises.

"And she's been a patient of Dr. Melvin's in Boston."

"She was seeing some guy down there. Dr. Worthy sent her to him. She was kinda depressed."

"And Dr. Worthy is?"

"Her gyno."

"Is he here in town?"

"Haverhill," Benedetto said.

"At Mary Murphy Hospital?"

"Yeah."

"When did this happen?"

"It was Thursday," Benedetto said. "Two Thursdays ago. I remember because she always seen the shrink in Boston on Thursdays so she'd be home late."

"And was she late that night?"

"I don't know. We had a softball banquet. When I come home I found her in bed."

"Can you tell me what made you call the police?" I said.

"She was all sweaty and her skin was pale and she felt cold and I couldn't hear her breathing."

"Did you tell the police she didn't do drugs?"

"Yeah."

"And?"

"They sort of shrugged. I figure they thought she did but I didn't know it."

"And nobody followed up?"

"Small-town cops," he said.

I nodded.

186

"I am very sorry you had to talk about it all again," I said. "It must be awful for you."

"It is," he said in his expressionless voice.

CHAPTER
FORTY-SEVEN

Dr. Figueredo was dark-haired and pale-skinned with the shadow of a close-shaved dark beard. He spoke with no accent.

"Figueredo is not a Puerto Rican name," I said.

"I am Brazilian," he said. "Why do you say that?"

"I was told you were Puerto Rican."

Dr. Figueredo smiled.

"We all look alike," he said. "What would you like to know about Sally Millwood?"

"You saw her when she arrived in the emergency room?"

"I did."

"Was she alive?"

"No."

"I know there was no autopsy, but could you speculate on what killed her?"

"My guess would be drug overdose."

"Because?" I said.

"Because I've seen a lot of them and you develop a feel. She was young, in good health, untraumatized, and died suddenly."

"But you have no hard medical evidence."

"Not without an autopsy."

"Could it have been suicide?"

"Of course it could, but usually there's a note or something. Most suicides don't really wish to go quietly into that good night," Dr. Figueredo said.

"Did you know she was seeing a psychiatrist?"

"No."

"Her gynecologist was a doctor named Worthy. Do you know him?"

"I know he's on staff here."

"And you didn't talk with him."

"Ms. Randall," Dr. Figueredo said. "We get people brought in here dead every day. We probably have ten drug ODs a week." He wasn't angry. His voice sounded a little sad. "We don't have much money and the administration is on our collective asses to keep costs down. What resources we have we devote mostly to the living."

"Seems the right choice," I said. "Do you know where Dr. Worthy has his office?"

"I'm sorry I don't," Dr. Figueredo said. "Check with the information desk in the lobby."

Dr. Worthy was a slight man in full country-doctor getup. White hair, gold-rimmed glasses, three-piece tweed suit, dark wing-tip shoes. He even had a gold watch chain across the middle of his vest.

"Thanks for squeezing me in," I said.

He smiled at me as he had smiled at a thousand women. *There there, dear, nothing to worry about*. But not a man to waste time.

"What can I help you with," he said.

"You were Sally Millwood's gynecologist," I said.

189

He nodded, smiling.

"You know she's dead."

He nodded again, looking sad.

"Did you send her to a see a psychiatrist?" I said.

"I guess confidentiality is not a serious issue here," he said.

"I know she was seeing him. Why did you send her?"

"She was depressed," Dr. Worthy said. "I tried her on Prozac for a while . . ."

He shook his head and shrugged a little. *What's a doctor to do?*

"And was it you who chose Dr. Melvin?"

"Yes."

"Why him?"

"I knew him," Worthy said. "We interned together at Mt. Auburn."

"Have you remained in touch?"

"No. It was just a name I knew. I looked him up in the phone book."

"So you don't really know him?" I said.

"Not really, just a man I knew casually twenty-five years ago."

"How'd you know he was good?"

"Well. He went to Harvard Med. He's licensed. Why wouldn't he be good."

That road led me nowhere so I turned off it.

"Did you know a doctor named Barry Clay?" I said.

"No, did he go to Harvard?"

"Just a thought," I said. "Do you have any idea why she might have been depressed."

"She said she was having trouble with her boyfriend."

"What kind of trouble?" I said.

"She didn't really specify, just that they weren't getting along and it was making her unhappy."

"Did you see her after she started seeing Dr. Melvin?"

"I don't really recall," he said. "I'm sorry I can't be more helpful, but . . ."

He stood.

"I do have an office full of patients," he said.

I thanked him and left. As I passed through his waiting room I saw that it was in fact full of patients. I was very glad I wasn't one of them.

CHAPTER
FORTY-EIGHT

Kim Crawford and I took Sam for a walk through West Concord. It was cold and rainy with a spatter of snow mixed in with the rain.

"I'm sorry, Kim, but I'm going to have to be a little more aggressive about you and Dr. Melvin."

"What?"

"Were you and he ever intimate?" I said.

"Excuse me?"

"Were you and he ever intimate?"

"Of course not."

The Akita paused to sniff at the base of a bush. We waited while he did so. Given the size of the Akita and the size of Kim Crawford, I'm not sure we had a choice.

"It would hardly be the first time it happened," I said. "Psychotherapy is an intimate undertaking. It happens a lot."

She shook her head. The Akita finished sniffing and we moved on.

"Dr. Melvin has been intimate with other patients," I said.

I didn't actually know that, though obviously he had been intimate with a former patient, Melanie Joan, and besides, detection is a lying business.

"He wouldn't," Kim said.

"Why wouldn't he?" I said.

"He wouldn't do that," Kim said.

Her eyes were beginning to tear up.

"To whom?" I said.

Kim's eyes were wet, and her lower lip trembled.

"He wouldn't do that to me," Kim said.

"He wouldn't have sex with you?" I said.

"He wouldn't with anyone else," she said fiercely.

"But you?"

"We were special," she said. Her ferocity was building.

"So you and he were intimate," I said.

She started to speak and stopped. She looked at me as if I were treacherous. Which, actually, I guess I was, a little.

"We were not," she said.

I nodded. We walked in silence for a short while. The Akita snuffling eagerly along among the wet leaves, the rain beading on his thick coat.

"Did Dr. Melvin ever give you any medication?" I said.

"Medication?"

"Yes. Maybe to calm your nerves? Help you relax?"

"No, of course not."

"Why of course not?" I said. "Lots of psychiatrists prescribe medication for patients."

"Well, John didn't."

"You called him John?" I said.

She stared at me without saying anything. The Akita seemed to feel something going on between us. He stopped and leaned against Kim's leg gently, and looked at me.

"I don't wish to talk with you any further," Kim said.

"Kim, if Melvin is exploiting you, and exploiting other women, he is doing just the opposite of what he's supposed to be doing. He's harming you."

"I want you to leave me alone," Kim said.

"Kim," I said. "We both know that you and he . . ."

She held up her hand. "Sam is trained," she said. "If you don't leave me alone I'll tell him to attack."

I had a gun. But I didn't want to shoot the dog. I kind of wanted to shoot Kim, but it would be hard to explain to the cops.

But Officer, she wouldn't answer my questions.

"Okay," I said. "I'll leave you alone. But please, for your own good, see another psychiatrist."

"Go away," Kim said.

"There's a doctor named Max Copeland. See him."

Kim shook her head. The Akita had stiffened a little. His ears had gone back. It was time. I turned and walked back toward Kim's condo where my car was parked. Kim didn't follow me. Which was just as well, because when I got there, I found the front windshield spray-painted black.

CHAPTER
FORTY-NINE

I called Julie and she came and picked me up.

"Who the hell would do such a thing?" she said.

I told her about the nude picture.

"It's dirty tricks," I said. "Maybe escalating a little. Joey Marino will come out and tow it. I assume they'll have to replace the glass."

We were on Route 2 in Lincoln. It was dark. Julie had the head-lights on. The rain/snow mix had turned to mostly snow as evening approached.

"I'm scared for you, Sunny."

I nodded.

"That would be the idea," I said.

"To make you scared?"

"Yes."

"Are you?"

I was quiet for a little while. "Well," I said, "already a guy came to my loft and threatened me."

"My God . . . threatened you how?"

"Floating facedown and naked in the Charles River."

"Sunny, my good Jesus."

"So I'm not sure paint on my windshield is so scary."

"You think it's the same ones?"

"Same three," I said.

"Three men?"

"Yes."

We passed over Route 128. In one direction the white headlights gleamed through the light snowfall. In the other an endless and receding pattern of red taillights showed.

"Is it Melanie Joan's husband?"

"And two friends," I said.

"Have you told the police?"

"Brian Kelly has the picture," I said. "He's running it through the forensics lab."

"But about the rest of it."

"I know it," I said. "But I need to prove it."

"Would you want to come and stay with me, you and Rosie?"

"You're sweet to offer, but I'll stay where I am."

We were heading in the right direction, toward Boston. The traffic was heavier heading away from the city. Across Route 2 the lights were all on in the low brick building where Raytheon had its headquarters. It looked cozy. Lighted windows in the dark through the snow always look cozy. How cozy could it be in the Raytheon headquarters?

"You never answered my question," Julie said. "Are you scared."

"I try not to think about it," I said.

"But you are."

"Of course I am. Only an idiot would be unafraid. But I try not to think too much about being afraid. I'm better off acting as if I weren't."

"Richie?" Julie said. "Spike? Your father?"

"And Brian Kelly and maybe Lee Farrell, and maybe every old boyfriend I ever had."

I shook my head.

"There's nothing wrong with asking for help, Sunny."

"Ever the social worker," I said.

"Everybody needs help sometimes."

"Jule, we've had this conversation. In fact I'm having it with everyone these days. And to tell you the truth I'm a little sick of it."

"I'm sorry," Julie said.

"You know, and I know, that I can't do what I have decided I want to do, and be the person I have decided I am, if every time I get scared I run to some man I know to bail me out."

We passed the big new Mormon Temple up on the right. The long legal wrangle had ended. The steeple was in place.

"You don't have to think of it as 'bailing you out,'" Julie said after a little while.

"However you wish to describe it," I said, "I experience it as being bailed out and I don't want that."

"Did you experience calling me to come get you as being 'bailed out'?" Julie said.

I started to say *that's different*, and knew she would say *different how?* and I would say *because you're my friend* and she would say *isn't Spike your friend, isn't your father even more than a friend, and aren't you and Richie friends?* And I would be required to say that too was different, and she would ask how and I didn't want to go there.

I said, "I made an exception in your case."

CHAPTER
FIFTY

I sat in my now-accustomed position beside the desk, facing Dr. Copeland, who had swung his chair toward me.

"For a woman who's not in therapy I spend a lot of time talking to psychiatrists," I said.

Copeland nodded.

"What you said about patients telling Dr. Ex of my interest?"

Copeland smiled faintly.

"Well, I guess they did, because one of his friends came and threatened me to stop questioning one of his patients."

"Threatened you how?"

"Implied physical threat."

"How did you react?"

"I pointed a shotgun at him and told him to leave."

Copeland smiled again faintly.

"It would seem to give weight to your suspicion of Dr. Ex."

"I think he's molesting his patients," I said.

Copeland cocked his head.

"My client, Melanie Joan, met him through therapy and later married him."

"Were they intimate while she was in therapy."

"Yes."

Copeland nodded.

"Another current patient denies intimacy so vigorously," I said, "and so unconvincingly."

"Tell me about her," Copeland said.

I'm a good observer and a good reporter. I told him in detail.

"Anything else?" Copeland said when I was finished.

"Another current patient of his died of a drug overdose."

"Woman patient?"

"They're all women patients."

"Were the circumstances suspicious?"

"It was a mediocre death in a small town," I said. "Nobody paid a lot of attention. There was no autopsy. But she had come from Dr. Ex and was dead in bed when her boyfriend found her. He says she didn't use drugs. There was no suicide note."

"Why was she seeing Dr. Ex?"

"Her gyno sent her because she was depressed."

"Any cause for her depression?"

"She was having trouble with her boyfriend."

"That's a good cause," Copeland said. "Did the police find any drugs in the house?"

"Not that I know of. But I'm not sure anyone looked. No one paid much attention to this girl."

"Except Dr. Ex."

"And she'd have been better off without it."

Again Copeland did his little half nod, encouraging me to talk some more.

"Tell me about date rape drugs," I said.

Copeland raised his eyebrows.

"There are a number," he said. "Versed, Rohypnol, GHB, Ketamine, something new called Burundang, which is a form of scopolamine. They all have the effect of pacifying the recipient so that she, or he, can offer little, if any physical resistance to sexual assault. Rohypnol is often called Roofies or roach, GHB is sometimes known as Liquid ecstasy or Cherry meth, Ketamine is known among other things as Special K, I'm sure Versed has a half dozen street names as well, but I don't know them."

"Could an overdose kill you?" I said.

"Under the right circumstances," Copeland said. "Do you think Dr. Ex administered such drugs to one or more of his patients?"

"Yes," I said.

"Do you have any evidence?"

"None that I could take to court," I said.

Copeland smiled. "Women's intuition?" he said.

I smiled back at him. "Something like that."

"Now, I'm afraid I'll have to know Dr. Ex's name."

I hesitated.

"I may have knowledge that will help you," he said. "And it may influence my own judgment of where to refer patients."

"Yes," I said after a moment. "You do have to know. His name is John Melvin."

Copeland had no reaction.

"Do you know him?" I said.

Copeland made a little head movement which indicated only that he'd heard me speak.

"Christ," I said. "I could ask you what time it is and you'd avoid answering."

"You find that annoying?" Copeland said.

"Oh Christ," I said. "Must you always be a shrink?"

"What would you like me to be?" Copeland said.

"Human?"

"You're not here to see me because I'm human," Copeland said. "When you came in you made a point of saying you weren't in therapy."

"A little humor, Doctor."

Copeland didn't say anything. I knew the technique. I had questioned enough suspects when I was a cop. Be still. Stay patient. And the suspect will find a way to say it.

"One of the odd things in my time with Dr. Melvin," I said, "was that we actually seem to be getting at things about me."

Copeland nodded.

"I suppose he could be a good shrink," I said.

"Or he has a good patient," Copeland said.

"I'm not his patient," I said. "And I'm not yours. I'm a detective on a case."

"What things are you getting at?" Copeland said.

God, he was relentless. I took a long breath.

"I seem to want to be with a man who is just like my father, but I don't want to be with a man who is just like my father."

Copeland smiled.

"My father took care of everything, my mother acted like she took care of everything. My father loved her unconditionally. If you asked my mother if she loved my father she would say "he'd do anything in the world for me." "

"And think she had answered the question," Copeland said.

"Yes."

"So you want a man who will take care of everything, and you want to be a woman who takes care of things herself."

"Yes."

"What has Dr. Melvin's response been."

"He's mostly interested in my sexual impulses."

If Copeland's face ever showed anything it might almost have shown a moment of disapproval.

"You find that inappropriate?" I said.

"I'm interested in emotional conflict," he said.

I felt a small shock of recognition. I had never thought of myself as someone with emotional conflict. Copeland was quiet some more. Then I smiled at him.

"Then have I got a girl for you," I said.

CHAPTER
FIFTY-ONE

It was dark with a small cold rain misting down. Rosie was taking her late evening walk and I was along to hold the other end of the leash. We got to the Summer Street Bridge, and looked at the black water in Fort Point Channel, and turned and headed back toward my loft. The street was empty. Past Melcher Street Rosie stopped dead and put her ears up. There was a stir of dark movement in the recessed entry of one of the big silent rehabbed warehouses that line that end of Summer Street. I unbuttoned my raincoat. As I did so, Rosie barked once and three men in ski masks and dark clothing stepped out of the entryway. I dropped Rosie's leash. The three men grouped me toward the wall, and one of them grabbed me from behind and pinned my arms. Another one pressed his hand over my mouth and the third man faced me with something in his hand. There was some sort of white glove on the hand.

In deference to the rain, I was wearing high-heeled black boots. I stamped a heel down on the toes of the man behind me, at the same time I bit the hand over my mouth. The hand went away. The man behind me grunted with pain and twisted to get his foot out of the way. It made him loosen his clamp on my arms a little and I was able to reach back with my left hand and grab a hard hold of his scrotum. I squeezed. He yelped and let go, trying to pull my hand loose. With my right hand, I fumbled under my raincoat. The man whose hand I had bitten hit me across the face with his fist. As I staggered I got my gun out from under my coat. I slammed it into his cheek, and put my back against the building and brought the gun up and pointed it at the third man, the one who had something in his hand.

"Drop it, you sonovabitch," I said.

The man said "gun" in a high panicky voice, and dropped what he had in his hand. The man to my right managed to hit me on the side of the head and I pitched sideways, with things popping behind my eyes. I hung on to the gun and rolled over onto my back and, with both hands on the gun, fired at all of them and none of them and anything that was in front of the muzzle. In the still wet darkness, the shot thundered among the silent warehouses and along the empty street. A man said, "Jesus," and the three of them ran for Melcher Street. I got to my feet with my balance still compromised and aimed at the running figures. Too far. They turned the corner at Melcher and I could hear their footsteps fading.

I started after them and had to stop and lean against the brick wall. I got steady enough to turn and look around for the something the man had dropped. I found it, and got down on my knees in the shiny street, and picked it up. It was a hypodermic needle. It had broken. I picked up the pieces carefully and put them in my purse carefully, and still on my hands and knees with my head still unsettled, I looked around. *Rosie*. There was no sign of her. *Jesus Christ*. I got my feet under me and stood and staggered a little and got myself balanced again, and moved along Summer Street, with my gun in my hand, balancing with my right shoulder against the brick front walls of the buildings. I found Rosie in the entryway of our building, her leash still trailing, humped up rather like a skunk in the fog, as my father used to say.

"Maybe I should have bought an Akita," I said to her.

She wagged and I went to my knees and hugged her, the gun still held in my right hand, while she lapped my face.

CHAPTER
FIFTY-TWO

I sat on the edge of a desk in the Homicide squad room in the new police headquarters with a homicide detective I knew named Lee Farrell.

"Lab says the stuff in the broken needle was a prescription drug called Xactil," Lee said. "They use it to tranquilize people before surgery, and, sometimes, as a muscle relaxant."

"Oh," I said. "That Xactil."

"Street name is Zack," Lee said. "In moderate dosages it gives you a nice high. More will render the recipient unconscious and an even higher dose will kill him . . . or her."

"How high a dose was in the hypodermic needle."

"No way to tell."

I bumped my heels gently against the side of the desk.

Lee said. "You know who they are?"

"Yes."

"Shall we go get them?" Lee said.

"I can't prove it. They had on ski masks. Were there prints on the needle?"

"Not enough surface intact," Lee said.

I bumped my heels some more.

"You want to talk about this?" Lee said. "I'd rather not explain to your father how I let you get killed."

I smiled at the image.

"Daddy would be hard to reason with, I guess."

"So?" Lee said.

"I can't, yet," I said. "I know a lot, but I can't prove any of it."

"Women's intuition?" Lee said.

I shook my head.

"Maybe your husband's family could be helpful," he said.

I shook my head again, my heels bumping gently against the desk.

"Are you suggesting something illegal?" I said.

Lee shrugged. "I don't want to see you get hurt," he said. "How about the big bear?"

"Spike?"

"Yeah."

"I am not ready to admit I can't handle this," I said. "If I'm going to do the work I want to do, I can't be running to some man to help me every time it threatens to get rough."

"Sunny," Lee said, "it has gotten rough. How about Phil?"

"My father?"

"Sure, he was a hell of a cop," Lee said. "He still knows how."

"I can't run to my father, Lee."

He nodded. "Me," he said. "On my own time?"

"Thank you, no. But I mean it," I said. "Thank you."

Lee shrugged. "There's nothing wrong with knowing what you can do and getting help when you need help," he said. "Would you ask for help moving a piano?"

"Not the same," I said. "I'm not in the piano moving business."

"Even piano movers don't usually move them alone," Lee said.

I smiled at him. "Oh shut up," I said.

"Ah," Lee said. "Now I get it."

CHAPTER
FIFTY-THREE

I took Rosie to stay with Richie again. I felt safer when she was there.

In my car with my brand-new front windshield, I brought Melanie Joan over to a large white ugly building on Soldiers Field Road, to talk with Joyce Kulhawik on Channel 4. After she was through and we were in the parking lot, Melanie Joan said, "Is there somewhere around here we can get lunch?"

"Across the river," I said.

"Cambridge?"

"Sure. How fancy do you want?"

"Oh," Melanie Joan said. "Just coffee and a sandwich."

We ate on Huron Avenue in a little place called Full Moon, near a drugstore and across from a bank. I had egg salad on wheat bread. Melanie Joan ordered tuna on white. We both had coffee.

"This is lovely," Melanie Joan said, "just what I had in mind."

I nodded.

"We need to talk," I said.

"Of course, Sunny."

"I need to know more about you and John Melvin," I said.

I watched her face close down.

"What more could you possibly need to know?"

"How did you and he begin dating?" I said.

"I told you. We met during therapy."

"Isn't that highly inappropriate?" I said.

"Oh pooh, you're starting to sound like a shrink," Melanie Joan said.

"We need to talk about this," I said.

Melanie Joan put her cup down so hard that coffee spilled onto the tabletop.

"I will not talk about it," she said.

She tried to wipe up the coffee with a small paper napkin and wiped a little coffee off the tabletop and into her lap. She tried to blot her lap, but the wet napkin fell apart. She started at it for a moment and then began to cry. It was loud full-out crying, the kind where your shoulders shake and you wail and have trouble catching your breath. I waited until she got her breathing under control. People in the restaurant looked at us covertly.

"How did you and he move from therapy to romance?" I said.

She was still sniveling with her head down. She didn't look at me. She shook her head.

"You've already told me," I said, "how he stood by and watched you being assaulted."

She nodded.

"How could this be worse to tell me?"

210

She shook her head. I waited. She didn't speak. I drank some coffee. Melanie Joan sat staring at her hands which were folded in her lap. She had stopped crying. I waited a little more. The waitress refilled our coffee cups, trying hard not to look at Melanie Joan.

When the waitress left, I said to Melanie Joan, "You're angry about the assault. But you're, what, ashamed about the romance?"

"Embarrassed," Melanie Joan said to softly that I leaned a little forward to hear.

"Because you feel foolish," I said.

"I disgust myself," she said.

I leaned even closer to hear her.

"Melanie Joan," I said. "I believe he tried to kill me." She nodded.

"He would do that," she said.

"I think he might have killed a young woman from Groveland."

"He could have," Melanie Joan said.

"If I can get proof that he did it, you won't have to worry about him anymore."

Melanie Joan had not moved. She kept her hands folded in her lap, her head down. Her coffee was unsipped in front of her.

"Why do I have to . . . Can't you catch him without me?"

"I need to know as much as I can about him."

"I will never testify in public," she said.

"Even if it would put him away?"

"I will never testify," she said.

"Okay," I said. "Can you at least tell me?"

She didn't answer.

"It might help me catch him," I said.

"I'm a famous person," she said. "I do not wish to become a tabloid joke."

"I won't tell anyone," I said. "I promise."

Melanie Joan stood up suddenly. She still didn't look at me. She put the wet balled useless napkin on the table.

"We'll do it in the car," she said.

She turned away quickly and walked out of the restaurant. I put a twenty-dollar bill on the counter by the cash register.

"Keep the change," I said to whoever could hear me, and went out after Melanie Joan.

CHAPTER
FIFTY-FOUR

"I had been married twice," Melanie Joan said, staring straight ahead as I drove along Huron Avenue, "and failed both times."

"I don't have a dandy track record myself," I said.

"You've only been married once."

"And had several failed affairs."

"That's because you won't let go of the first marriage."

I shrugged.

"Do you want children?" Melanie Joan said.

"I think so."

"And the clock is beginning to tick," Melanie Joan said.

I smiled at her, though she was still staring at Huron Avenue and I don't think she saw me.

"Could we talk about John Melvin?" I said.

"And I went to see Dr. Melvin because I heard that he was especially good with women in my situation."

We stopped at Fresh Pond Parkway and waited for the light.

"He was wonderful. I talked. He listened. Do you know how enticing that is, to have a man listen?"

The light changed and I turned left onto the parkway.

"Did you ever have a man listen to you?" Melanie Joan said. "Really listen?"

"Richie listened," I said. "But when I got through with whatever I was saying, he would say that I should do what I wanted to."

"And you didn't like that?" Melanie Joan said.

"Partly," I said. "Tell me more about John Melvin."

"I shared with him some of my fantasies. He helped me see that without a man in my life I feared being abandoned. And with a man in my life, I feared being controlled."

We went past Mt. Auburn Hospital and curved around the head of the Charles toward Soldiers Field Road.

"And then, one session, about three months after I started seeing him, he stood up from his desk where he sat and came around and stood behind me and put his hands on my shoulders. And started to massage my shoulders. I guess I tensed a bit. It was so unexpected. He said I was very stiff and tight. He said I should lie on his couch and he would give me something to help me relax. I was hesitant."

Melanie Joan spoke slowly and carefully and formally, as if she were giving a seminar.

"He told me that the heart of any therapy depended on a bond of trust between the patient and the therapist, and that I needed to trust him."

We passed Channel 4 again, and passed the Harvard Stadium complex. Girls in plaid skirts were playing field hockey. Melanie Joan was becoming more and more lost in the story she was telling. I was so silent I barely breathed.

"So I lay down on the couch, and he gave me an injection."

She stopped. I could hear her breathing.

"I could see and hear and feel," she said.

I waited, listening to her breathe. She stared straight ahead through the windshield. The car seemed as if there were too much air in it. Melanie Joan seemed to be inside herself now.

Her voice, when she spoke again, was very small and soft, and uninflected.

"It's not so easy to undress someone who is just lying there. While he did it, he told me that because I trusted him, I could allow him to control me completely. And doing that, I would overcome my fears."

"And?" I said, finally.

"And then he took off all his clothes."

I waited. She didn't speak or look at me.

"And?" I said.

Her voice shook as she spoke.

"And he fucked me," she said.

It was where I had known we were going. The river on our left, with the sun shining on it, looked cleaner than I knew it was. There were joggers on the esplanade, jogging on sanely. There were dogs, and Frisbees. The traffic was light on Storrow Drive. Across the river, on Memorial Drive, it was even lighter.

"Why didn't you tell the police?"

She shook her head.

"It became a regular part of our therapy," she said.

I went off Storrow Drive at the Kenmore exit and pulled in on a hydrant around the corner on Bay State Road. I turned in the seat and stared at her. I tried to speak gently.

"You let him do it again?"

"I liked it," she said.

CHAPTER
FIFTY-FIVE

The car trembled faintly as the motor idled. Across the street from where we sat was the former hotel, now a dorm, where Eugene O'Neill had died. Melanie Joan was now looking right at me. *Okay, I've told it to you, now what are you going to do with it!*

"That's why you're so afraid of him," I said.

She nodded.

"You're afraid you'll give in, that you'll let him do it again."

She nodded. I was silent.

"What was it you liked?" I said after a while.

"The Master Slave thing," she said.

My mouth was dry. I felt the way I had felt in Melvin's office the day I had cried. I wanted to cry now. Something fearsome and misshapen had jumped suddenly out of the dark and hissed.

"And you married him," I said.

"I did."

"But things changed?"

"Not at first."

"Did he . . . I'm sorry. It's not something I need to know."

Melanie Joan smiled without any hint of pleasure.

"I've started," she said. "You may as well get it all. Yes, even after he married me he still gave me a shot."

"Do you know what it was?"

"The drug? Xactil," she said.

I didn't know quite what to ask her. I knew what I wanted to know, but I had gotten so deep into the bottom of her psyche that I wasn't sure what I had a right to ask.

I settled finally on, "So what happened?"

"The Zack wasn't enough," Melanie Joan said. "We started to do . . . other things. And after a while they weren't enough and he wanted to pass me around to his friends."

The ultimate control.

It had begun to rain a little. Not very hard, a small misting rain that gathered on the windshield, and made the pedestrians, mostly B.U. students, hunch up a little. The cars passing us had their wipers on intervals. Most had their headlights on. I decided not to ask what the other things were.

"Whatever we had done before, and I knew it was sick, but it was a sickness we shared, it was just the two of us. When he wanted to share me with his friends I felt devalued."

I might have felt devalued sooner than that. But each to her own pathology.

"And the friends were Dirk Beals and Barry Clay?"

"Yes."

If she testified against any of the men, her own craziness would be on display. She was famous enough

218

to become, eventually, a joke in Leno's opening monologue.

"And Melvin would watch."

"Yes."

"Did this ever consummate?"

"No. The first time it happened was when I ran away."

"You weren't drugged," I said.

"No, I think it made him feel more powerful to simply require it of me, without Zack."

The rain no longer misted on the windshield. Now it coalesced and slid tangibly down the glass. The B.U. kids hurried as they walked, hugging buildings when they could. Umbrellas had appeared. Hoods were up on sweatshirts.

"And you never told anyone?" I said.

"No. I had no one to tell."

"You need help with this," I said.

"I have you."

I reached across and patted her hands where they lay folded in her lap.

"You need more than me," I said.

CHAPTER
FIFTY-SIX

"Xactil," Dr. Copeland said, "is often used as a preoperative tranquilizer. Or for certain procedures where the patient needs to be relaxed and pain-free but responsive to directions."

I was in his office, sitting in the chair, leaning toward him, with my clasped hands pressed against my chin.

"Is it dangerous?"

"An overdose is lethal," he said.

"Is there much margin for error?"

"Some," Dr. Copeland said. "But an overdose is not unheard of."

"What's the result of an overdose?"

"Pallor, cold sweat, respiratory impairment, loss of consciousness, death."

"Is it always injected?" I said.

"No. Injection is the fastest-acting, and probably the most precise in terms of dosage. But it can be taken by mouth in tablet form, by intranasal spray, or in suppository form."

"John Melvin has injected at least one patient with Zack," I said. "And had sex with her."

"You know this?"

"I know this."

"Then he should have his license revoked," Copeland said.

"I think he has done this with more than one patient."

"These things are very rarely one time only," Copeland said. "Can you prove that he did this?"

"To my own satisfaction," I said.

"More than that?"

"No."

"That's not enough for me to take to the licensing board," Dr. Copeland said.

"Nor for me to put him in jail," I said. "I think he OD'd one of his patients."

"Fatally?"

"Yes."

"What is your evidence?"

I was silent.

"What is said in here does not leave here," Dr. Copeland said.

I told him about Melanie Joan.

"And the patient who died?"

I told him about Sally Millwood.

"Autopsy?"

"The mother refused," I said. "Though maybe she could be convinced to change her mind."

Dr. Copeland shook his head.

"Zack only lasts a few hours in the system," he said.

"I also think he tried to kill me," I said.

Dr. Copeland raised his eyebrows, which, I had come to learn, was an indirect invitation to say more. I told him about Dirk Beals, and about the attack on the street.

"And still you pursue him," Dr. Copeland said.

"I do," I said.

"I cannot make unsubstantiated charges against a colleague even if I believe they're true."

"And you do?"

"I would tend to believe things you told me," Dr. Copeland said.

I almost blushed. We sat together quietly. Dr. Copeland seemed capable of perfect stillness for any length of time. He reminded me of Richie that way.

"Is there an antidote?" I said after a while.

"Yes. Dilazaplin."

"How is that administered."

"Normally, it is injected. But like Zack, there are formulations for oral, nasal, and rectal administration."

I sat back. Copeland watched me as if everything I did were a clue.

"Can it be taken preventively?"

"So that if you are administered Zack it won't work?" Dr. Copeland said.

"Yes."

"I think so, but we are reaching the limits of my pharmacology. Before I would say yes or no I'd have to consult a specialist."

"Do you have one in mind?" I said.

Dr. Copeland nodded.

"I do," he said. "I'll call him."

"And let me know?"

"Call me tomorrow," Dr. Copeland said.

222

He sat a little forward in his chair and folded his hands on the edge of his desk.

"I will remind you of something you certainly know," he said. "If any of this is true, you are dealing with a dangerous man."

"I know," I said. "But I have a big edge on him."

Again the raised eyebrows.

"He'll hold me in contempt because I'm a woman, and it will make him underestimate me."

"As long as you don't underestimate him," Dr. Copeland said.

He shifted slightly in his chair and half glanced at his watch which I now knew was the indirect way of saying the fifty minutes were up. I stood.

"A funny thing," I said.

He cocked his head.

"When Melanie Joan told me about the control business between her and Melvin . . ."

I stopped. He waited.

"I . . . it still bothers me."

He nodded neutrally.

"Maybe when this is over I should look into that a little."

Dr. Copeland nodded his head slowly and smiled slightly.

"Maybe," he said.

I hesitated at the door for a moment, then I opened it and went out.

CHAPTER
FIFTY-SEVEN

I called Spike from my car.

"As soon as I hang up," I said, "get over to Melanie Joan's, and stay with her."

"Okay."

"Melanie Joan doesn't leave her apartment without you," I said. "Not for a minute, not with anyone else. I don't care who. She leaves her apartment, you are with her."

"Okay."

"Do you still have that big, icky .45?" I said.

"A classic," Spike said. "Colt. Government issue."

"Carry it," I said.

"For John Melvin?"

"And friends," I said.

"I've seen John Melvin," Spike said. "I don't need a gun for John Melvin."

"Carry the gun," I said. "These guys are dangerous. They made a run at me, and I think they killed a girl in Groveland."

"You going to tell me about it?" Spike said.

"Not now. I have to think. I'll tell you later."

"I don't like him making a run at you," Spike said.

"Me either," I said. "If he makes a run at Melanie Joan you can kill him."

"I'll keep it in mind," Spike said.

When I hung up with Spike I looked at my dashboard clock. It would be ten past ten in Los Angeles. I called Tony Gault.

"Tony Gault's office."

"Is Tony there?"

"Who's calling please."

"Sunny Randall."

"I'm sorry, Ms. Randall, Mr. Gault has just stepped out of the office. May I take a message."

"You may," I said.

"I'm sure he'll call you right back."

"Tell him not to do that," I said. "Tell him, instead, to take a flying fuck at a rolling donut."

"Excuse me?"

"A flying fuck," I said. "At a rolling donut."

And I hung up the phone.

My head felt like a blender. I wanted to collect Rosie and go somewhere. I called Richie. His machine answered.

"It's me," I said. "I'm going to stop by for Rosie."

Richie had a condo in a recycled warehouse on one of the Commercial Street wharfs. From his living room you could watch the harbor. I parked in the visitors slot and rang his bell. In a moment he opened the door. Except it wasn't he. It was her. I stared at her. She stared back.

"May I help you?" she said.

She was great-looking, for a floozie, and she looked nothing like me. Her hair was thick and dark. Her face was oval and her eyes were very big. She had a wide mouth with tiny smile lines at the corners. She was wearing a white terrycloth robe. But her hair was combed and her makeup was exactly right.

I said, "I've come to pick up Rosie."

"Oh." She smiled. "You must be Sunny. Come in. I hope this isn't awkward."

I went in and she closed the door behind me. Her feet were bare.

"I'm Carrie LeClair," she said. "Richie is working."

I nodded, and put my hand out. "Sunny Randall," I said. "Where's my dog?"

"Rosie's on the couch looking at the view," she said and started to show me.

"I know the way," I said.

We went into the living room. Rosie was sleeping on a big couch that faced the vast picture window that looked out on the gray harbor where the boats glided by. She opened her eyes and looked at me. Then sat bolt upright and stared. Her tail began to thump against the couch.

"Hello, my little twinkle," I said.

She jumped off the couch and dashed around my ankles then back to the couch and up and off and around my ankles and the length of the living room and back and chased her tail. I sat on my heels and put my arms out and she ran over and lapped my face and chased her tail again and sat down suddenly and looked at me.

226

"Rosie and I have had a lovely time," Carrie said.

"Isn't that swell," I said.

"We take a lovely walk," The Floozie said, "every morning along the waterfront. She gets a lot of attention. Everyone loves her."

She sat on the couch, and tucked her robe around her knees. Her legs were very good.

"Would you care for coffee?" she said.

I could shoot her. I had my gun in my purse. Or I could shoot me. I hated how good-looking she was. How good her legs were. I especially hated how nice she seemed.

"No . . . thanks. I need to be going."

"Well, it was good to meet you. Bye-bye, Rosie."

Rosie, the treacherous little turd, went over and jumped up on the couch beside The Floozie, and settled down. Maybe I should shoot Rosie. I took her leash from my big purse and went over and snapped it onto her cute red nylon collar. Rosie jumped down in anticipation of a walk, her tail wagging a blur. We went to the door. The Floozie stood and smiled and walked to the door with us. I opened it.

The Floozie said, "Bring her back anytime. I love having her here. We get along really good."

I stood in the hall with the door still open and one hand on the knob and looked at her for a minute, thinking about my gun.

Then I said, "It's ten minutes to one in the afternoon, lady. Get fucking dressed," and closed the door and took Rosie to the car. By the time I got there

227

the small part of me that wasn't enraged and jealous was embarrassed.

I put Rosie in the car on the front seat.

"Didn't I handle that well," I said to her, and closed her door and went around and got in my side and drove away.

CHAPTER
FIFTY-EIGHT

"You slut," I said to Rosie as we drove on 128 toward Gloucester. "You little round heels. You'll roll over for anyone that will pat your belly and give you a cookie."

Rosie was lying on the floor in front of the passenger seat with her nose poked up into the heater opening. I had long ago tested it on my hand and been satisfied that she couldn't get her nose far enough up there to get nicked by the fan. She seemed to be paying no attention, the little traitor.

My sister owned a summer home in Gloucester, near Wingaersheek Beach. Elizabeth didn't use the house in the off season, nor, in truth, very much in the on season. She valued it mostly because it had been pried away from her ex-husband, as part of the divorce settlement.

I parked in the empty driveway and walked Rosie down to the beach and let her off the leash. She went like a torpedo for about a hundred yards straight down the beach, and stopped and stared at the water and trotted down to it and stood as it rolled in and barked at it.

The day was bleak. It wasn't so cold that we couldn't stand it, but there was a wind off the water and the sky was low and dark, and drizzling. I had on an ankle-length black wool coat with a big collar. I turned the collar up and buttoned the coat to the neck and stuck my hands in the side pockets. The water was the same color as the sky, and they merged somewhere infinitely far out where there no longer seemed to be an up or down. I walked slowly along the beach, watching Rosie dash and stop and sniff and spin and dig. There were a couple of gulls and she froze when she saw them. They hopped around paying her no attention until she charged them, at which time they soared disdainfully into the air and glided away. Rosie stood looking after them, with her tail wagging furiously.

There was something about the ocean with its ceaseless movement and its blank entirety that made me feel as if I were looking at eternity. I could feel its movement. I could feel my mind begin to mingle with the movement and the sound and smell and look of it. I could feel the hard clench of my self begin to loosen.

I felt as if Melanie Joan and I had blended a little bit. I was afraid of John Melvin, too. It made me mad. I knew Melvin was a monster. I was sure that Melanie Joan wasn't his only conquest. I was convinced that he had killed Sally Millwood with an overdose. I was sure he and his two friends had been behind the ski masks. I didn't know if they intended to kill me or drug me. If they had drugged me, what would have happened? It made the inside of me feel a little bit jagged. Drugged was somehow scarier than killed. I had a fearful flash of myself immobilized before them. I shook my head. I needed to put this away. Maybe I should tell Richie. He would speak to his father and in a little while Uncle Felix . . . I smiled on the cold beach . . . I enjoyed the image of Melvin confronting Felix Burke . . . for a moment it made me feel good . . . But only for a moment . . . I remembered almost regretfully that if I were to be relieved of whatever this was, I was the one that needed to do it.

Rosie found a ratty tide-mauled tennis ball, and brought it to me in her self-important trot. I threw it for her and she chased it madly.

I thought about Richie . . . I thought about Brian Kelly and Tony Gault . . . I thought of men I'd slept with . . . I liked men . . . I felt as if I had been enveloped by the gray wind on the personless shore beside the evocative ocean . . . I thought about my mother and father . . . The beach stretched uncluttered and empty for miles. There was no one but Rosie and me. I stood for a while and listened to my breathing. I watched Rosie scooting around the beach, her nose near the sand. I looked at the ocean and looked at the ocean and after a while I called Rosie and we went home.

CHAPTER
FIFTY-NINE

I called Dr. Copeland. I got his service and left a message and in forty minutes he called me back. Well ahead of Tony Gault.

"I've talked to Dr. Chou," he said. "At Mass General."

"And?"

"Theoretically," he said, "there's no reason that Dilazaplin, taken shortly prior, shouldn't prevent the effects of Xactil."

"Theoretically?"

"Normally it is administered to reverse the effects of Xactil when those effects are no longer needed," Dr. Copeland said. "There has been very little reason to investigate its preventive effects."

"But it should work."

"It should," Dr. Copeland said.

"How long will it be effective?"

"It would need to be taken shortly before the Xactil was administered to have its full potency. Or promptly afterwards before the Xactil set in."

"How shortly?"

"Five minutes, ten at the outside."

"Side effects?"

232

"Some people feel nausea from conventional dosages of Dilazaplin," Dr. Copeland said.

"And taking it the way I suggest?" I said.

"It should not make any difference."

"How big a dose would I need?"

"It would depend on how much Zack you received," he said.

"Enough to make someone conscious but immobile."

"Is the someone you?"

"Say it is."

"You are what, about a hundred and twenty pounds?"

"Around," I said.

"So the Zack dosage would be about five milligrams. The Dilazaplin would be two point five milligrams."

"And it can be given in a tablet?"

"Yes it can."

We didn't speak for a moment. The open connection between us made its non-noise.

"Can you prescribe some for me?" I said.

"Are you planning to use yourself as bait?" Dr. Copeland said.

"Yes."

"You understand the danger," he said.

It wasn't a question. I didn't answer.

"The danger would be heightened," Dr. Copeland said, "if he were to discover that Sunny Randall and Sonya Burke are one and the same."

I didn't say anything.

He said, "You are swimming in uncharted waters, Sunny."

I felt a little thrill. He had used my first name. Why was that thrilling?

"And," he said, "no one can guarantee that the antidote taken before the sedative will prevent its effect."

"But you think it will," I said.

"I think it will. But there's insufficient science to prove it."

"Melvin is a monster," I said.

"Yes," Dr. Copeland said.

"Will you give me a prescription?"

"Yes."

CHAPTER
SIXTY

A state police detective named Meyer came to call on me. I offered coffee, he accepted, and we drank it at my dining nook in the bay window of my loft. Rosie joined us.

"What the hell is that?" Meyer said.

"That's Rosie," I said.

"Did you trap her?"

"Of course not."

"I got possums in my grape arbor," Meyer said. "She looks like one of them."

"She absolutely does not look like a possum," I said. "She is a purebred miniature English bull terrier and an unusually attractive one."

Meyer shrugged and scratched Rosie behind her ear. He drank some coffee, took a lemon square, had a bite, and chewed thoughtfully. He was gray-haired, and clean-shaven, and pushing sixty, though he seemed to be in good shape.

"You're Phil Randall's kid," he said.

"One of them," I said.

"I done business with Phil over the years. How's he doing?"

"He's retired," I said. "Seems to like it."

"He make captain?" Meyer said.

"He did."

"Phil was a wonderful cop," Meyer said.

"Yes," I said.

He drank some more coffee, swallowed, and ate the rest of his lemon square.

"Got a dead body out in Concord," he said.

I felt stiff inside.

"Concord?" I said.

"Yeah."

"Probable cause?" I said.

"ME says heart failure, but she was only thirty-three years old. We just want to be sure he's right," Meyer said.

The stiffness had spread. It was hard to speak.

"What brings you to me?" I said carefully.

"You were the last entry on her calendar."

"Kim Crawford?" I said.

"Yes."

"Autopsy?"

"Inconclusive," he said. "Does rule out heart failure. Doesn't demonstrate it."

"Drugs?"

"No sign."

"Needle marks?"

Meyer looked at me without speaking for a moment.

"Coroner didn't find any," he said.

"Tell him to look again."

"You know something," Meyer said.

"I do. It's a case I'm working on."

"Tell me about it."

"There are no facts," I said, "that will help you."

"Impressions help," he said. "Suppositions help. Suspicions help. Sometimes when we have those we find the facts."

"And sometimes you don't," I said.

"And sometimes we don't," he said. "I know you used to be on the job."

I raised my eyebrows, the way Dr. Copeland did.

"I called your father before I talked to you."

"I'm sure you meant well," I said. "But I'd prefer to be treated as Sunny Randall, instead of as Phil Randall's daughter."

Meyer looked tired. He smiled slightly.

"It wasn't about you," he said. "It was about Phil."

"Yes," I said, "of course it was. I take it back."

"Fine," Meyer said. "Tell me about your case."

"The thing is," I said, "is that I am working on a suspect undercover. I'm close. If he finds out about me, we lose him."

Meyer nodded.

"And," I said, "I have a client who will be badly damaged if we don't handle this right."

Meyer nodded again.

"Well," he said. "Usually I blab everything I know to anybody I can find, but being as how you're Phil Randall's daughter, I'll keep it to myself this time."

I nodded.

"Okay," I said. "Okay."

"So?" Meyer said. "Talk to me."

I did.

"And they didn't autopsy in Groveland."

"No. She'd used drugs in the past. When her boyfriend found her she was maybe still alive, or very recently dead, and she was still displaying OD symptoms."

"And this Xacwhatever, it leaves no residue?"

"Xactil," I said. "You never heard of it?"

"Nope. Roofies, I know. G-Juice. Special K. But No Xactil."

"State of the art," I said. "It doesn't leave a trace."

"You think this doctor might have injected her?"

"She could have been a witness," I said. "If I ever get him to court."

"Would the dog have known him?" Meyer said.

"I don't know. Why?"

"Almost took the arm off the first Concord guy that responded. Wouldn't let anyone near her. They had to finally get the dog officer and dart him."

"Where's the dog now?"

"Ex-husband."

"That weasel."

Meyer shrugged.

"Dog was glad to see him," he said.

"Any port in a storm," I said.

"Should I look into him?"

"No. I doubt he's anything worse than an asshole."

"Lot of that going around," Meyer said.

"If Kim had let the doctor in and welcomed him, the dog would have let him alone," I said.

"You want to tell me the doctor's name?" Meyer said after a moment.

238

I didn't want the cops in it yet. Meyer was probably good at his job. But it was too delicate. If Melvin got scared, he'd close down like a trunk lid and I'd never catch him. And I wanted the son of a bitch, for everything he'd done to women, including scaring me. I didn't like being scared.

"Not yet," I said.

Meyer looked at me for a while.

"And you've got nothing that would let us arrest him," Meyer said.

"Intuition," I said. "Circumstance, things people have told me that they won't repeat in public. The way he acts with me. But absolutely nothing that could get you an arrest warrant. Nothing."

Meyer stood and went to my kitchen counter and poured himself some more coffee and came back and sat down and stirred in sugar and skim milk. Rosie stayed seated by his chair, but she turned her head to watch him. One never knew when food might appear.

"I need to be the one," I said.

Meyer sipped his coffee.

"Well," he said. "Being Phil Randall's daughter gets you something."

"Thank you."

"But not everything," Meyer said.

CHAPTER
SIXTY-ONE

I called Richie in the morning.

"Are you alone?" I said.

"Yes," Richie said. "Carrie's not here."

"May I come over?"

"Of course."

I opened my mailbox on the way to the car and took out my mail. Folded the long way, so it would fit, was another manila envelope. In the manila envelope was another picture. Another naked woman, lying on a couch. It might have been the same one. Again she had my face, and this time someone had drawn a slash mark across her throat with a red Magic Marker. It was clumsy. But it made my stomach tighten.

I put the envelope in my bag and took Rosie to where I'd parked my car. I felt as if I were being looked at. We got in. I started up. And we drove to Richie's without incident. When we came in, Richie picked Rosie up and kissed her on the nose and rubbed her stomach while we walked to his living room. When he put her down she jumped onto the couch and sat on her tail and looked at both of us expectantly. Still standing, I took the picture out of my purse and handed it to him. He looked at it for a long time. Then he put it down on the coffee table. I thought maybe the lines around his mouth had deepened a little.

"I know the face," he said. "I don't know the body."

"It's my head pasted on, of course."

"Yes."

"I need your help with this," I said.

"Really?" Richie said.

"I'm scared," I said.

"Good to know," Richie said.

"That I'm scared?"

"That you can admit it," Richie said.

"I'm working on that," I said. "Will you help me?"

"Of course."

Richie's stillness was comforting.

"You know about Melanie Joan Hall and her husband," I said.

"What you've told me," Richie said.

"I think he has killed two women," I said. "I think he routinely drugs and rapes his patients."

Richie's expression didn't change as I told him everything I knew. His gaze stayed on me as I talked — almost tangible, as if I would still feel it should I look away.

"So you can't prove any of it," he said when I finished.

"No."

"Why not tell the cops what you think and let them see if they can turn something up?"

"I'm afraid they'll fail and it will just warn him."

Richie nodded.

"I could make this go away pretty quickly," he said.

"No," I said.

"Sometimes the wrong thing for the right reason isn't so bad a thing," Richie said.

"I do not want my problems solved by your gangster family," I said.

"Because you disapprove of gangsters?" Richie said. "Or because they've scared you and you have to vindicate yourself."

"Maybe both," I said.

"But you'll take help from me."

"Yes."

"Because I'm not a gangster."

"Yes."

"And?" Richie said.

"And because I trust you," I said.

"And you trust me because?"

I didn't answer for a minute.

"Because I think you love me," I said.

I was aware of my breathing. Rosie sat expectantly on the couch watching us. Richie nodded slowly.

"I got coffee made," Richie said. "You want some?"

"Yes," I said. "Skim milk and two Equals if you have it."

"I know," Richie said.

He went out of the living room. I stood for a moment looking after him, feeling as if I were on some kind of emotional balance beam. Then I sat on the couch and put my arm around Rosie. In a few moments Richie came back carrying coffee in two large white mugs. He kept his in his hand and put mine on the coffee table in front of me, next to the pasteup nude

242

with my face. Then he sat on the couch on the other side of Rosie. He put his arm around her as well, and when he did his hand brushed mine.

"So," he said. "What are we going to do?"

CHAPTER
SIXTY-TWO

On the fourth Sunday of every month, Emma and Phil
Randall invite their two daughters for dinner. They still
lived in the square white six-room Colonial house my
father had bought on a not very fashionable street for
$17,000 in 1959. He and my mother had slept upstairs
in the modest front bedroom, and my sister Elizabeth
and I had been in the other two very small bedrooms.
Elizabeth, being older, had gotten the one with two
windows. It was the fourth Sunday, and there we were
having cocktails in the living room. My parents' idea of
a cocktail was Jim Beam bourbon over ice. It had no
effect on my father, but my mother was drunk by the
time she finished the first one. Elizabeth and I were
having wine.

"I was playing bridge with the girls," my mother said.
"And I bid two no trump and made it. And Florence
Goddard said to me, 'Emma, I never saw anyone get
more out of a hand of bridge than you do.' "

I didn't play bridge, and I didn't know what it meant
to bid two no trump and make it.

"You are a wonder," my father said, with no hint of
irony.

Elizabeth apparently did know what two no trump was, or pretended to.

She said, "That's not so hard to make, Mother."

"It certainly is," my mother said.

With every milligram of bourbon that went in, she became more certain of everything.

"It certainly is, especially if you are playing with the partner I had."

"Be kind, Emma," my father said. "They can't be expected to play like you do."

"I know," my mother said, "I know. And Millie is a love."

Did he really think she was a good card player? Or was it all part of the family pretense that my mother was not a dope?

"I don't really have much time anymore to play cards," Elizabeth said and smiled at Daddy. "Now that I'm dating."

"And there's all that tennis," I said.

"If you'd had a better lawyer," Elizabeth said, "you'd have time to play tennis, too."

"I didn't want alimony," I said.

"I still don't understand," my mother said, "what happened to your marriage, Elizabeth, either of you as a matter of fact. If you had come to me, and we had talked, I'm sure I could have straightened the whole thing out."

I saw Daddy smile a little.

"Emma," he said. "Is it okay if I check the chicken?"

"Oh pooh to the chicken," she said.

Daddy smiled again and stood and headed for the kitchen. I wanted to go with him.

"Phil," my mother said, "get me another little drink, would you?"

Daddy took her glass as he passed. Too bad he couldn't make the drink weaker, I thought, but bourbon on the rocks is sort of hard to water.

"Not too much ice," she said.

I always suspected she drank bourbon on the rocks so it would be hard to water. She looked after Daddy while he was getting the drink.

"What's going on in there, Phil?" she said.

I knew Daddy was adjusting the oven to keep the chicken from overcooking. My mother didn't cook well, and my father was in fact responsible for much of the food preparation. But we all maintained the fiction that my mother did it. I'm not sure she even knew that she didn't.

My father came back with her drink and a bottle of white wine from which he freshened up my glass and Elizabeth's.

"How many drinks have you had?" my mother asked.

"Mother," Elizabeth said, "this is my second glass."

"It's not good for young people to drink a lot," my mother said. "Old bones like mine need a little drink-y, but youngsters like you . . ." She shook her head. "How many have you had, Sunny?"

"I've lost count," I said.

"Oh you think you're so smart," she said. "Phil, how much has Sunny had to drink?"

"A glass and a quarter," Daddy said, "since she arrived. But we don't know what she did before she got here."

My mother's face got a pained look. It was a look I'd seen all my life. It meant she was afraid.

"Well," she said. "They're both at a very vulnerable age."

"Mother, I'm thirty-eight," Elizabeth said.

Elizabeth had never learned to roll with it.

"Vulnerable age," my mother said. "Vulnerable age."

She drank a third of her bourbon. Always about now, I wished that my father would slap her and send her to bed. And always I was disappointed that he didn't.

Elizabeth and my mother fought awhile about just what was and was not a vulnerable age. I watched my father. He seemed to be with us, but what was said seemed to have no effect on him. He was pleasant and courteous and kind and probably far away inside himself where he had always lived.

After a while we had dinner. The chicken was okay. But the baked potato was shriveled from cooking so long, and the frozen winter squash was still cool in the center.

CHAPTER
SIXTY-THREE

"I don't know what's wrong with my father," I said.

I was in my Sonya Burke getup, sitting with both feet on the floor, my knees demurely pressed together.

"Because?" Dr. Melvin said.

Today he was in a perfectly cut blue suit with a very white shirt, ruby cuff links, wearing a black, red, and gold paisley tie.

"He never . . . he never stands up to her."

"Your mother?"

"Yes."

"Why would you want him to?"

I thought a minute. I was trying to pretend during the therapy session that I didn't know what I knew about Melvin. I tried to steer it where I wanted it to go, but I tried to do so with real issues dredged up from my real situation. He was good. I was afraid that if I were inauthentic, he'd catch me.

"To protect me."

Melvin smiled and nodded.

"From your mother," he said.

I nodded.

"But if he did?" Melvin said.

"If he did, what?" I said.

"If he became your ally against your mother. If you and he became the couple in the family . . . ?"

We were silent while I rummaged around in my psyche, or tried to in such a way as to take this Melvin where I thought he was ready to go. Melvin sat quietly looking at me pleasantly enough, but with a hint of I-know-and-you-don't in his expression. That was probably a no-no for a shrink, and the first time I'd seen anything in his face.

"Oh shit," I said after a time. "It's Oedipus again, isn't it?"

Melvin smiled and his expression intensified.

"You were not, as a child, prepared to replace your mother in your family," Melvin said. "The thought would be terrifying."

"And, symbolically," I said, "I still am?"

Melvin raised his eyebrows. We were quiet. I began to nod my head slowly.

"Yes," I said. "I still am. That's it, isn't it?"

"There may not be an *it*," he said. "But that might certainly be an aspect of your pathology."

"Pathology?"

"It's the accurate word," Melvin said. "It needn't frighten you."

"Pathology," I said. "I have a pathology."

"After all, most people do," he said, "who come to see me."

I sat quietly for a time.

Then I said, "What are we going to do about it."

I floated the "we" out there on purpose. I wanted to see if he rose to it. He leaned back in his chair for maybe thirty seconds, gazing at me. It was the look that made me feel as if I were sitting there naked and he were reviewing my assets.

"How much do you trust me?" he said.

I didn't want to seem eager. I hesitated, thinking it over.

"How much?" I said.

He nodded gravely.

"I trust you completely," I said.

He smiled and stood up and walked around behind my chair and put his hands on my shoulders.

"You're very tight," he said and began to massage my shoulders and neck. I felt my stomach clench like a fist.

"Relax," he said gently.

I breathed carefully, conscious of the tightness in my shoulders, thinking about relaxing them.

"That's better," he said. "Feel better?"

"Yes."

"We need a little more time," Melvin said.

I nodded, focused on relaxing.

"I have a full schedule today, but I could see you Thursday evening."

"Evening?" I said.

"Yes. I reserve Thursday evenings," he said. "Not everyone can be in a rigid schedule of fifty-minute hours."

I nodded. Simple Sonya. Trusting, relaxed, feeling safe with my doctor.

"Can you come?" he said. "I am pretty sure I can help you take a big step."

"Yes," I said softly. "Yes I can come."

"Good," he said. "Seven-thirty. Come in as you always do."

"And you'll come from your office," I said. "And get me."

He rubbed my shoulders a little more.

"Yes," he said, "just as I always do."

"Okay," I said.

In my head was a line from a song my father used to listen to when we were driving someplace: *I'm gonna go fishing and catch me a trout*. I think it was a movie theme song. Mel Torme was the singer. I almost smiled.

I'm gonna go fishing and catch me a trout.

CHAPTER
SIXTY-FOUR

When I left Dr. Melvin I drove straight for Melanie Joan's condominium. I called Richie in transit.

"Thursday night," I said.

"Okay," Richie said.

"I'll come by this evening and we'll talk about it," I said.

"Okay."

"Is Rosie all right?" I said.

"She's fine."

There had been a light snowfall the previous night, less than an inch, but it was enough to make things white.

"Is she loving the snow?" I said.

"Yes."

Richie was never chatty. I gave my car to Melanie Joan's doorman and called her from the lobby. She was waiting in the doorway when I got out of the elevator. She was wearing blue sweats and a maroon tee shirt with Harvard on the front. Her hair was done, and her makeup was in place.

"Is Spike here?" I said when we were inside.

"No," Melanie Joan said. "Today I'm in all day reading galleys."

"Good," I said. "We need to talk."

"About what I told you?" Melanie Joan said. "I can't talk about that."

"I need you to fill me in," I said. "With details."

"I don't want to."

I got up and walked across her vast living room and stared down into Copley Square. Then I turned and stared at her.

"Listen," I said. "We have a chance to put him away. To take him forever out of your life. But I need you to talk to me."

Melanie Joan was looking past me out the window. She shook her head.

"Yes," I said. "You are going to talk to me. He's made your life a mess. He's attempted to hurt me. He may have killed two women. We have a chance to put the sonovabitch in jail. And we are going to take it."

Her gaze shifted from the middle distance onto my face. We looked at each other for a moment, then she stood and went to her bedroom. Was she going to go in and lock the door? No. She returned almost at once with a small amber prescription bottle.

"Ativan," she said.

She went to the refrigerator, took out a bottle of Volvic water, shook two pills into her palm and took them with the water.

"Ativan is a tranquilizer?" I said.

"Yes."

We went back to the living room. And sat down.

"Wait a little while for the Ativan to work," Melanie Joan said. Despite her careful makeup, her face looked very pale. "How is Rosie?"

"She's fine," I said. "I've left her with my ex-husband for a while."

"In order to work on my case."

"Yes."

"Are you afraid for her safety?"

"Not while she's with my ex-husband," I said.

"Spike said he was going to check up on his restaurant," Melanie Joan said, "but, to tell you the truth, he doesn't seem very worried about it."

"Spike worries about very little," I said.

"He's quite outrageous," Melanie Joan said.

"Quite," I said.

"But good company."

"Very," I said.

I wasn't too chatty myself. We sat quietly for a little longer. Something about Melanie Joan's face began to soften. I couldn't quite figure what it was. Something about the eyes.

I said, "The first time he raped you."

"I never really thought of it as rape."

"The first time he injected you with a paralytic substance and had sex on you," I said.

"You make it sound so awful."

"It is awful," I said.

She nodded.

"The first time," I said. "Where did it happen."

"In his office."

"How did you come to be there at night?"

"He told me that he needed more time with me," she said. "He told me that sometimes therapy wasn't always possible in the rigid fifty-minute hour."

If it works, keep using it.

"And the time all three of them tried to rape you?"

"Same thing. In his office."

"Where in his office?" I said.

"Where?"

"On the couch, on the floor, on the desk? Where?"

"On the couch."

"Did you have a handbag?"

"A handbag?"

"Did you have one?" I said.

"I suppose so. I always carry one, don't you?"

"What did you do with it?"

"I don't know."

"Think back."

Melanie Joan lowered her head again and moved it slowly back and forth. I didn't think it meant *no*.

"Take me through the night," I said. "Step by step."

Melanie Joan kept looking at the floor, her head swaying slowly.

"He began to rub my neck and shoulders," she said. "He told me I was tight and needed to relax. He said "Do you trust me?" I said I did. He said I should lie on the couch and he'd give me a shot of something to relax me. He said the therapy wouldn't work if I was 'tight'."

"This is the first time you and he had sex."

"Yes."

"Go ahead."

"So I said, "All right" and I lay down on the couch. I remember I felt funny, lying on the couch." She paused and tossed her head slightly once, then back to the back and forth. "I remember being very modest as I lay down, very careful with my skirt."

"What did you do with your handbag?"

She was silent for a time.

Then she said, "On the floor. I put it on the floor beside the couch. And he gave me a shot and I did relax and then he began to . . . to feel me up."

I waited. She didn't speak.

"And?" I said.

"And he undressed me. The bottom half. He left my top on. And . . ." She shrugged. "And then he did it."

"And you were aware?"

"Yes."

"But you couldn't move?"

"No. I felt so relaxed all I could do was lie there."

"Could you speak?"

"I don't know. I didn't try to."

"Did he disrobe?"

"Yes."

"Entirely?"

"Yes. For God's sake, why are you digging at me? You're like a voyeur."

"I need to know," I said.

"I can't go much further."

"Not much further to go," I said. "What happened when it was over?"

"He put his clothes back on, and went back to his desk and sat and looked at me."

256

"Did he say anything?"

"Not then. After a while I could move and I got up and put my clothes back on. And he said I had been right to trust him, and that having such an experience with a man I totally trusted would take me a long way toward recovery."

"How long after the shot did it start to work?"

"Maybe five minutes."

She stood and walked to the other end of her living room and back and stood in front of me.

"I can't anymore. I won't talk anymore."

"That's fine," I said. "You don't need to."

CHAPTER
SIXTY-FIVE

We sat at a round, glass-topped table in Richie's kitchen, while Rosie slept on the couch in the living room.

"What if the Dilazaplin doesn't work?" Richie said.

"I'm assured that it will," I said.

"On Xactil, yes. What if he uses something else?"

"You rush in and save me."

"And how do I know whether you need saving or not?"

"That's one of the things we need to figure out," I said.

Richie nodded and leaned back in his chair with his hands clasped behind his head. His arms were very muscular. That wasn't anything new. Why was I noticing it now? Why was I thinking about why I was noticing it? Maybe I should see a psychiatrist.

"I need to know the layout there," Richie said.

"We'll walk through it," I said. "It will help me visualize."

"Visualize," Richie said.

"Sorry," I said. "I've been seeing a lot of shrinks lately."

"Pretty soon," Richie said, "you may be seeing one less."

"I hope," I said.

We stood and walked into the living room. Rosie was snoring. She opened her eyes long enough to see that we were doing nothing that involved a ball or a cookie, and closed them again and resumed snoring.

"His house faces the street. A big Victorian with a front porch."

"Two stories?"

"Two plus an attic. There could be rooms in the attic. The office is in the back. There's a path . . ." We began to walk across the living room. I turned right past the coffee table, and opened an imaginary door. "I go in."

"The door's unlocked?" Richie said.

"Yes. There's a small waiting room and a stairway. The office is on the second floor."

"How do you know when it's time to go up?"

"He comes to the top of the stairs and says 'come on' or some such."

"Can he see the whole waiting room from the stairs?"

"No. Over here is out of sight of the stairwell."

"Okay," Richie said, "so he says 'come on' and you go up."

"The stairwell turns at a landing." I walked back across the living room, gesturing directions with my open right hand. "At the top of the stairs there's a hall, you turn right" — I did — "and go in his office." I took two steps and stopped. "He holds the door for me and closes it when I come in. His desk is sort of right there" — I gestured slightly to my right — "and he sits and I sit facing him in a chair. The couch is behind me."

"How's the room run?" Richie said.

"What do you mean?"

"I mean is it more or less an extension of the hall or is it like the cross of a T?"

"T," I said.

"Tell me about the hall."

I closed my eyes, and gestured. "Runs down to the left. Door at the end. Door to the left of the stairs. Door across the hall."

Richie got a Bic pen and a yellow pad of blue-lined paper from a drawer.

"Draw it," he said.

I sat at the table again and sketched it out. "The drawing is pretty bad," I said.

"It is," Richie said. "Where's the couch in his office?"

"To the left when you enter."

I pointed with my pen.

"And what's in this room?" Richie said.

He was talking about the room across from the stairs.

"I don't know," I said.

"Does the door have a lock?"

I stopped and closed my eyes.

After a moment I said, "No."

"What's going on with the rest of the house?"

"I don't know."

"Anyone live there?"

"Not that I could see."

"I'd be happier," Richie said, "if you were wearing a gun. Or a wire. Or both."

"You'd be happier if you could sit in the room with me, and so would I," I said. "But I've got to let this guy go far enough to trap him, and I'm afraid he'll discover them if I wear either one."

"You're going to let him paw you?"

"I'm going to let him incriminate himself," I said. "I'll go as far as I can stand."

Richie blew his breath out softly, and rubbed his thick hands together.

"Me too," he said.

CHAPTER
SIXTY-SIX

Rosie stayed at Richie's. I went home and didn't sleep very much. Wednesday morning, Meyer the state cop came by just after breakfast.

"Where's your dog?" he said.

"Vacation."

He nodded. "The ME went over Kim Crawford's body again, with a magnifier."

"And?"

"You were right. There was a small puncture wound."

"Where?" I said.

He didn't look at me.

"In her . . ." He paused, looking for the language. "Hidden by her pubic hair," he said.

"Was she clothed when you found her?"

Meyer shook his head.

"In bed," he said. "Naked. Covers over her."

"And the dog?"

"Lying on the bed beside her with his head on her hip."

"Any sign she had sex before she died?" I said.

"No."

"The son of a bitch," I said.

Meyer raised his eyebrows at me. The technique seemed to be spreading.

"He went there and convinced her they were going to make love and when she had her clothes off and was on the bed he jabbed her with a needle."

"Instead of," Meyer said.

"Yes," I said. "Then he got up and put on his clothes and probably patted the dog and walked out and in a little while she died."

"He might have waited to be sure," Meyer said.

"In which case he got up and got dressed and sat and watched her die before he patted the dog and walked out."

"We can't prove the puncture wasn't self-administered."

"Would you stick a needle into yourself down there?"

"Jesus, no."

"I wouldn't either," I said.

Meyer leaned forward on my sofa with his elbows on his thighs and his hands clasped. The posture made him tip his head back a little to look at me.

"So now we don't have a probable heart attack," he said. "We got a probable murder."

I nodded.

"I can't give you much slack on a probable murder," Meyer said.

"I know."

"What's the doctor's name?"

"Give me another day's worth of slack," I said. "I'll bet the ME's report hasn't even been formally submitted yet."

"Another day?"

"Till Friday," I said. "I'll give you everything I've got on Friday."

"That's two days," he said.

"Not counting today," I said. "Just give me Thursday."

Meyer's clasped hands bobbed between his thighs. His head nodded slightly in the same rhythm. He sucked on his lower lip. Then he smiled.

"Okay," he said. "You give me everything you got on Friday."

"Promise," I said.

"Sure," Meyer said.

He took a card from his shirt pocket and handed it to me.

"Anything comes up, give me a call. If there's a collar in this, I'd just as soon make it."

"I'll call you first," I said.

"Remember to tell your old man that Normy Meyer was asking after him."

CHAPTER
SIXTY-SEVEN

I went to the South End to see Spike.

"Want some hot chocolate?" Spike said.

"Hot chocolate?"

"Yes. I make it from scratch."

"I may have never had hot chocolate made from scratch."

"It's time," Spike said.

I sat at the kitchen table in Spike's condo while he melted chocolate in a double boiler.

"When you say scratch," I said, "you mean scratch."

"I'm tired of Nestlé's Quik," Spike said.

"My mother's recipe," I said.

Spike nodded, stirring the chocolate carefully with a wooden spoon.

"Other than hot chocolate and the chance to admire my physique and wish I were straight," Spike said, "what brings you over the channel?"

"I could straighten you out," I said.

"In your dreams," Spike said. "Whaddya want?"

"I need somebody to take care of Rosie," I said. "If anything happens to me."

"Wouldn't that be Richie?"

"If anything happens to me and Richie."

Still stirring, Spike turned his head and stared at me.

"You're going to make a move on that fucking doctor," Spike said. "Aren't you."

I nodded.

"And Richie's going to help you."

I nodded.

"And it's dangerous."

"It might be," I said.

He nodded thoughtfully. "If I were going to do something dangerous," Spike said, "I'd just as soon do it with Richie."

"Yes," I said.

"Sure, of course," Spike said. "I'll take Rosie. She loves me. I love her. She'd be fine here."

"She'd miss her mommy," I said.

"For a while, but she'd adjust."

"Yes."

"Can I help you with the dangerous thing?" Spike said.

"No. Thank you. But I need you to stay with Melanie Joan, all day, tomorrow, including tomorrow night and Friday until you hear from me."

"So the deal is Thursday," Spike said.

"Yes."

"And if I don't hear from you?"

"Rosie is at Richie's condo. I'll give you the address and a key."

"Okay."

"And tell Richie's father that whatever happened is John Melvin's fault."

266

Spike turned back to his hot chocolate, pouring a thin stream of milk from a pitcher into the double boiler while he continued to stir with the wooden spoon.

"Which," he said, stirring gently, "would be the end of John Melvin."

"He can't be allowed to continue."

"I'll bet you could make that arrangement with Desmond Burke, without risking your ass."

"No," I said.

"Cop's daughter," Spike said.

"It's more than that."

"I know," Spike said. "I know."

CHAPTER
SIXTY-EIGHT

I got through the rest of Wednesday and all day Thursday, but not happily. Thursday evening I drove to Richie's condo at twilight. It began to drizzle, and the hint of snow that had fallen earlier was washed away. Everything glistened: the headlights on the wet streets, the red taillights, the gleam of moisture on the red brick buildings. I had become silent as the time approached. My whole self was still. My breathing was easy. My heart beat quietly. My mind was nearly blank.

When I got there, I stashed my suitcase, and Richie and I took Rosie for a walk along the waterfront. Rosie trotted self-importantly ahead of us. The rain wasn't hard enough to discourage her. We were quiet at first.

"You're sure you want to do this," Richie said after a while.

He was wearing a leather jacket and a black Chicago White Sox hat. The drizzle was persistent. We walked past Lewis Wharf.

"I need to do this," I said.

I was in black too, a trench coat with the collar up, jeans and boots, a wide-brimmed felt hat to keep my hair dry.

"No gun, no wire," Richie said.

"No," I said.

There was a thick black ornamental chair along the water, anchored to upright granite blocks. Rosie stopped to examine one closely, sniffing the full circumference of the granite.

"I run into a locked door," Richie said, "I'm going to kick it in."

"Yes," I said.

"I'm not taking any chances with you."

"I know," I said. "I want to catch him, but I don't want to get raped or killed or both to do it."

Satisfied with what she had learned from the granite post, Rosie moved on briskly.

"He might have his friends with him," I said.

"I figure I went to a tougher school than they did," Richie said.

Again we were quiet. When we reached the Marriott, we turned and began to walk back toward Richie's condo.

"Just remember," I said. "These are sick and dangerous people."

"I know."

It was dark now. The drizzle was beginning to turn to rain, which Rosie didn't like. She looked back at me anxiously, then picked up the pace toward home.

"I told my uncle Felix," Richie said, "that if anything happened to us, Melvin did it."

I smiled. Richie saw me in the ambient light of the city.

"What are you smiling at?" he said.

"I told Spike to tell your father the same thing."

"What did he say?"

"He said we could probably arrange to have your family do something about this without taking any risk."

"We could," Richie said.

"I can't," I said.

"I know," Richie said.

Rosie was at full tether now, with the drizzle now fully turned to rain, heading home as fast as she could drag me.

"I don't think I could do this without you," I said.

"It's good you don't have to," Richie said.

"It's kind of a relief." I said. "To tell you I need help."

"It's kind of a relief to hear it," Richie said.

CHAPTER
SIXTY-NINE

We were in my car. It was 7:20. We had come early so we could cruise the neighborhood around Melvin's office. I was in my Sonya Burke outfit again. Tonight I had chosen a plaid skirt and a demure white blouse. I took some gum out of my purse and peeled a stick and began to chew it.

"There's the Porsche," I said.

"You're sure."

"I remember the plate numbers," I said.

"So it's a gang bang," Richie said.

At 7:25, I stopped around the corner, out of sight of Melvin's house. We looked at each other for a moment. We'd gone over it many times. There was nothing to say. Richie put his hand out. I took it and we held on to each other for a moment. Then he closed the door and I drove around the corner and parked in front of Melvin's office. I took the gum out of my mouth and wrapped it around my Dilazaplin tablet and tucked it up inside my cheek.

When I went into the waiting room, I made sure the door was unlocked, and put a strip of duct tape over the latch tongue to keep it that way. The lights inside made the outside darkness more implacable. There was

271

a white-noise machine. There were back copies of *The New Yorker* on the small reading table between the two waiting chairs. I didn't look at them. I sat with my purse in my lap and my knees together and my ankles crossed, like an actor imagining herself into character. I breathed slowly and deeply, trying to relax my shoulders. The whooshing made by the white-noise machine underlined the stillness. I concentrated, saying Richie's name to myself. *Richie Burke, Richie Burke, Richie Burke*. As always I heard no footstep, he simply appeared at the top of the stairs.

"Come on up," he said, as he always did.

I went up the stairs, turned at the landing, reached the top. He stood by the door and gestured me through and came in after me and closed the door behind him. Did it lock? I went to my usual chair and Melvin went and sat at his desk as always. He tilted his chair back a little and smiled at me.

"Should I talk?" I said. "Like a regular session?"

"Usually," Melvin said, "you talk and I listen."

He smiled some more. He was such an attractive man. His smile was reassuring.

"Today," he said, "it's my turn for a moment or two."

I nodded. "Of course," I said.

"We have discovered, you and I, and, by the way, you've done impressive work here, that, as is the case with most girls, the first man in your life was your father."

I nodded. Purse in lap, hands folded, knees together, ankles crossed, lean forward a little. Look enthralled.

"Usually the strong presence of the mother prevents you from realizing any fantasies you might have about possessing the father. Which, of course, if realized would be terrifying."

I nodded five times to show I understood completely.

"In your particular case your mother's inadequacies, which you fully perceived, and which you knew from observation that your father perceived as well, made the actual attainment of the father frighteningly possible."

"Not in fact," I said.

"No, not in the phenomenological fact, but to your unconscious, a very real possibility."

I nodded some more. The light was dawning.

"So while you very much wanted and needed your father's care and love, you learned that you had to keep him at arm's length, and invented a way of doing so."

"And I transferred that push-pull to my relationship with all men."

"Exactly," Melvin said and sat back a little while I thought about it.

"Yes," I said. "Yes, that's right. I know it is. I know it not just rationally but, but . . ."

"Somatically," he said.

"Yes."

"Good."

We were quiet for a moment, then he let his chair come forward and leaned toward me a little with his forearms resting on the arms of the chair, and his hands clasped in front of him.

"To break that pattern," he said, "you need to trust a man, entirely. Do you trust me?"

273

"Yes."

"Completely?"

"Yes."

"Good," he said. "What I want you to do is lie on the couch for me."

I stared at him for what seemed the right amount of time, then, without a word, I stood and went and put my purse on the floor beside the couch and lay down. *Richie Burke, Richie Burke, Richie Burke.*

"Good," he said. "Now can you disrobe for me?"

"Disrobe?"

"Yes."

I was looking at the ceiling. It had been plastered with repetitive circular swirls.

"All . . . all the way?" I said.

"Yes."

"I . . . Doctor . . . I . . . Why do you want me to disrobe?"

"You need to trust me," he said.

"But I'm too embarrassed."

"I know," he said. "It's understandable. Let me give you something to relax you."

"Relax?"

"Yes. You'll be awake. You'll know everything that happens but it will make you calm and responsive to the therapy."

"You think I need to do this?" I said.

"If you're able to do this," he said, "I think we can break this circle of ambivalence once and for all, tonight!"

274

I was still for a time, looking at the ceiling swirls. Then I took in a long breath.

"All right," I said. "If you think I should."

"I do."

"Okay."

He stood and I heard him moving about the room. While he did that, I poked the Dilazaplin tablet out of the gum and onto my tongue.

"Give me your arm," he said and I did.

He swabbed a patch with alcohol.

"This won't hurt," he said. "Little pinch."

I felt the needle jab and swallowed my tablet. Melvin's voice deepened.

"There, just lie quiet, in a short while you'll feel the relaxation spread slowly through you."

I lay still. I felt a little shaky in my chest, which was probably tension. Otherwise I felt nothing. He stood quietly watching me. I let my eyelids droop and watched him through the slits. I saw him run the tip of his tongue along the surface of his lower lip.

"How are you?" he said.

I spoke slowly, trying to sound thick-tongued.

"I'm kind of sleepy," I said.

"Good," he said. "That's to be expected. Could you raise your right arm for me?"

I thought of what I had learned about Xactil and its effects. It was enough time. I stirred my arm slightly then let it lie still.

"Can't," I said.

"That's fine," Melvin said.

His voice was as deep and soothing as butterscotch sauce. Through my slitted eyes I thought his face looked a little moist. Maybe perspiration on his upper lip. He stepped to his desk for a moment and the office door opened and two men came in. I knew it would be Dirk Beals and Barry Clay. It was.

"She all set?" Beals said.

"Yes."

Clay came and looked down at me.

"How you doing, toots?"

I opened my eyes and looked up at him and said nothing.

"She can hear us," Clay said.

Melvin said, "Certainly."

"And see us."

"Yes."

"But she can't move," Beals said.

"That's correct," Melvin said.

The three of them gathered around the couch and smiled down at me. I looked up at them and didn't move. Melvin's face was definitely moist. I could hear all three men breathing.

Melvin said, "We have a special treat for you, Sonya." His voice was husky.

"Lean back," Beals said, "relax, and enjoy the flight."

The three men laughed and began to undress. They took off all their clothes, Melvin folding his neatly and putting them on his desk. The other two men let them lay where they dropped. Naked, the three of them formed a semicircle around the couch where I could see them. Being naked didn't make them look better.

276

"Three wise men," Clay said. "Bearing gifts."

Because I didn't want to move, I wasn't entirely sure that I could. But I felt entirely alert, so I was hopeful. I wondered if Richie was close. I knew if I didn't appear in fifty minutes, that he'd come after me. I'd been in the office maybe twenty minutes. A lot could happen in the next thirty. The three men posed, as it were, arrayed around me. There was something communal in their corruption, as if each helped the other to enjoy the adventure. All for one and one for all.

"Your turn, now, Sonya," Melvin said.

I shifted my eyes toward him and then to the others. He took the hem of my skirt and pulled it up to my waist. His face was red and sweaty now. The other two men looked flushed as well. All of them were excited. I could feel the tension along every nerve path. My legs felt rigid. So did my shoulders and neck. My chest was tight. I was having trouble getting in enough air.

"Good legs," Clay said.

"Like a rainy day," Beals said.

"You want to see them clear up."

"Badda bing," Clay said.

Both men giggled.

"It is time," Melvin said. His voice was very hoarse. "Time to be free, Sonya."

"Time to get fucked, Sonya," Beals said.

Melvin looked at his two pals. And smiled.

"Gentlemen," he said. "If you would."

He stepped back to watch. It was almost choreographed. They'd done this before. On either side of me, Clay and Beals each hooked a thumb under the waistband of my panty hose. It was as far as I could go. I drove my elbow into Beals's approximate crotch and rolled off the couch on his side where my purse was.

As loud as I could, I yelled, "Richie." And took my gun from the purse and held it in both hands and pointed it at Melvin. I felt myself tremble.

Beals hunched over in pain. Clay and Melvin stood as if in a stop-action film frame. The door to Melvin's office opened and Richie came in with a gun in his right hand and a small videocamera in his left. He looked at me for a long few seconds, then he raised the videocamera and filmed the three men, standing naked.

"You," he said to Beals. "Look up at the camera."

Beals remained bent over. Richie put his gun in his holster, stepped carefully behind me, and took a handful of Beals's hair. He yanked Beals's head up and shot ten seconds' worth of his face in close-up. Then he let him go and stepped back around me.

"You okay?" he said.

"I'm fine," I said.

"They get far?"

"They pulled my skirt up," I said.

Richie nodded. "Which one's Melvin?" he said.

"The distinguished-looking gentleman by the desk, with the silly-looking little penis," I said

Richie put the videocamera down on the couch beside me and walked across the room to Melvin. He stopped in front of him, standing so close that their bodies nearly touched. He stared into Melvin's eyes for a moment. Melvin looked back.

"You don't understand," Melvin said. "This is a therapy . . ."

Richie hit him on the point of the chin with his left hand. It was a short punch, but Melvin fell back over his desk and banged into his swivel chair and sent it rolling across the room. Melvin landed on his side on the floor. I felt the visceral release of it as if I had hit him myself. Richie went to the door and leaned on the jamb and rubbed his knuckles, his eyes on the other two men. Lying naked on the floor, Melvin looked pathetic. He began to whimper.

"I'll give you money," Beals said. "I have a lot of money."

Richie stared at him.

"I have a lot of money," Beals said.

In a clenched voice, Clay said, "I do too. I'll give you some, just let us go."

Richie looked at me. "You want to take their money?" he said.

"No."

"I'll testify," Beals said. "I know all about John. I'll tell you."

"He arranged all this," Clay said.

"The ship appears to be sinking," Richie said.

"And the rats are leaving," I said.

"I can tell you everything," Beals said.

Still holding my gun I went to Melvin's desk and picked up his phone and dialed a number I had memorized for this moment.

"You'll have your chance," I said.

The phone was answered on the second ring. "Homicide."

"Detective Meyer," I said. "Norman Meyer."

CHAPTER
SEVENTY

"I need to stay here tonight," I said to Richie when we got to his place and had spent enough time greeting Rosie so she had settled back down on the couch.

"Sure," he said.

"Any problem with Carrie?"

"I've put Carrie on hold while this was going on."

We were standing at his big picture window looking at the harbor. Some sort of patrol boat with a blue light on the stern moved silently across the black water.

"Because?"

"Because you needed help."

"I don't want to sleep with you," I said.

"There's a guest room," he said.

"It doesn't mean I never want to sleep with you."

"I know," he said. "How do you feel?"

"Vulnerable . . . dirty . . . frightened . . . angry."

"I would think," Richie said.

"I feel like I want to stay all coiled in on myself, you know? Like an armadillo."

"Yes."

A tanker moved its five-story bulk soundlessly across the harbor headed for the storage terminals along the Mystic River.

"When I was in there, after the shot, I didn't know if I could really move. You know. I had to keep still to pretend and I didn't know when it came time to stop pretending . . ."

"I came up right behind you," Richie said. "I was in that little room at the top of the stairs. With my ear against the wall."

"Could you hear?"

"I heard you yell," Richie said.

I shivered. "And if you didn't?"

"In twenty-eight more minutes I'd have come in."

We were both quiet. The tanker moved slowly. It was far away and silent, gliding like something huge and fearful across the nearly motionless water. Richie put his arm around my shoulder.

"You look like Meg Ryan," he said. "And you're tougher than my uncle Felix."

I felt myself shaking a little as if I were cold. I felt cold.

"Sit on the couch with me and Rosie," I said.

"Sure."

I sat and put Rosie in my lap. Richie's shoulder touched mine. He put his arm around my shoulder. I cuddled Rosie. We didn't speak for a while.

"I couldn't have done it without you," I said.

"Sure you could. You did. You had them compromised and your gun out when I got there. All I did was take some pictures."

"And hit Dr. Melvin."

"And hit Dr. Melvin," Richie said.

"Whether I needed you to subdue them, I don't know. Maybe not. But when I was in there and he shot me with the needle and I was on the couch, all I could do was think about you. I kept saying your name. Richie Burke. Like a chant."

"Backup is good," Richie said.

"I couldn't have gone in there without knowing you were close by."

"You didn't have to."

"Meaning?"

"Maybe you could have if you had to."

"I was very scared," I said.

"Me too," Richie said.

"For me?" I said.

"I didn't know what I was walking into."

"But were you scared for me?" I said. "Specifically."

Richie nodded slowly in the dim room. "That I'd fail you," he said. "I was afraid that I'd fail you."

CHAPTER
SEVENTY-ONE

Spike sat on the floor of Melanie Joan's apartment and threw the ball for Rosie. Rosie chased it the length of the big living room and skidded past it and picked it up and trotted back and dropped it in front of Spike and Spike threw it again.

"So what will happen," Melanie Joan said.

"Well," I said. "They attempted to restrain me chemically."

"Even though you weren't really helpless?"

"Their intent was to hold me against my will. That's illegal. They exposed themselves to me. That's illegal. I was administered medication against my will. That's illegal."

"But what about the murders? How will you prove the murders? Or when they tried to kill you?"

"The cops and the DA will try to flip somebody," I said.

"Flip?"

"Bargain with one of them to testify against the others."

"Will that work?"

"These don't seem to me like stand-up guys," I said.

"Will they bargain with John?"

"No."

"So he'll go to jail."

"After Beals and Clay rat him out?" I said. "He'll be in jail long enough so that you won't have to worry about him again."

"Will they let him out on bail or anything?"

"I doubt it," I said. "A known stalker accused of two murders. We'll stick with you until we know."

From the floor, Spike said, "So I guess my days here are numbered."

"In fact," I said.

"Does that mean I can stop throwing this fucking dog the fucking ball, soon?" Spike said.

"Shhh, she'll hear you," I said.

"Relentless," Spike said.

He rolled the ball down the carpet again.

"I can be alone," Melanie Joan said.

"As much as you want," I said.

Melanie Joan frowned. "I'm not sure I want at all," she said.

"There's nothing to be afraid of anymore."

"I know. It's just that I've been afraid so long . . ."

"You can't get rid of it," I said.

"No."

"You will."

"Will I see you anymore," Melanie Joan said. "Or Spike?"

"Of course," I said. "We've become friends, haven't we?"

"Yes."

"Friends see each other," I said.

Melanie Joan said, "Spike?"

"As long as you don't start touching me," Spike said.

Melanie Joan smiled.

"That's a tough condition," she said.

"I know," Spike said.

Rosie dropped the ball in front of him. He didn't throw it. She picked it up and dropped it again.

"Jesus," he said and rolled the ball once more across the carpet.

"I'm terrified," Melanie Joan said.

"Maybe you need to talk with a shrink," I said.

"That's what started me being terrified," Melanie Joan said.

"Think of it as the hair of the dog that bit you," I said.

CHAPTER
SEVENTY-TWO

I sat with Dr. Copeland in his office.

"The three of them," I said. "In a giggling semicircle, showing me their peepees."

Copeland nodded.

"I'd have been mortified if I were them, they? Whatever. To behave like that in front of friends . . ."

"Maybe the friends were part of the point," Copeland said.

"Strength in numbers?" I said.

"It might have been a way to access each other sexually."

"You mean they wanted to show each other their peepees? And I was just the excuse."

"That's a little simple," Copeland said. "Most actions are driven by more than one thing. But sometimes men with a repressed homosexual urge will have sex with the same woman as a kind of secondhand fulfillment."

"So the three of them having sex with me would, in a manner of speaking, be like having sex with each other."

"At least symbolically," Copeland said.

I thought about that. Copeland waited calmly.

"What about his medical practice?" I said.

"Isn't he going to jail?" Copeland said.

"Yes. I'm sure he will. But if he gets out earlier than he should. Could he practice psychiatry again?"

"I think we can see to it that he does not," Copeland said.

"Good," I said.

Again we were silent. Again Copeland was patient. All the time in the world. If we didn't get to it this time we'd get to it next time. If there was a next time.

"I couldn't have done what I did," I said, "without Richie's help."

Copeland nodded.

"The bond between you is powerful," he said.

"It is," I said. "Isn't it?"

"I don't know where it will lead, but you are obviously still connected."

It was what I had always thought. Now it had been certified, stamped yes. I sat quietly and looked at the yes from every perspective. It was a large, attractive yes. I nodded, more to myself than to Copeland.

"Melanie Joan is having trouble with this," I said.

Copeland tilted his head again.

"If I can get her to come, will you see her?"

"Yes," he said. "If she wishes to come, have her call me."

"I'm not certain I can get her to call you. Maybe I could arrange it and bring her?"

"If she hasn't the commitment to call," Copeland said, "she won't have the commitment to come."

"Do I hear a cliché about to surface?" I said.

He smiled slightly. It made me feel triumphant.

"You do," he said. "Unless she wants help, she can't get it."

"And calling you would be the first sign of commitment."

"Yes."

"Okay," I said. "Should I advocate?"

"Haven't you already?"

"Yes."

"Then she knows what you think."

"So it's up to her."

"It is," Copeland said.

"What if she doesn't come?"

"If she needs it badly enough, she'll do it," Copeland said.

I nodded slowly. Everything he said seemed so reasonable and why-didn't-I-think-of-that? On the other hand that had been true of Melvin when I was Sonya Burke.

"You know what's sort of funny," I said.

He tilted his head and raised his eyebrows a little and waited.

"When I was seeing Dr. Melvin, and I knew he was a rapist and probably a murderer, he still helped me see things about myself."

"Being corrupt doesn't make him incompetent," Copeland said.

"No. But . . ."

"You are also very quick and intuitive," Copeland said. "You have a very fine mind."

"I didn't think I was going to get into this when I came," I said. "I thought I was coming to fill you in on what happened with Melvin, and to see if you were willing to help Melanie Joan."

"I'm sure you had those reasons, too," Copeland said.

"We've talked about this before."

"Yes."

"It has to do with my father and mother," I said.

Copeland smiled, bless his heart, and said, "How unusual."

Then he shifted a little in his chair and glanced at his watch.

"Time?" I said.

"I'm afraid so," Copeland said.

"Am I still scheduled at this time next week?"

"Yes."

"Maybe I should come back," I said.

"Maybe you should," Copeland said.

"We'll talk," I said.

Outside, the day was not very cold for January. A thin snowcover melted in the winter sun. There were some squirrels in the trees. I looked up at the sky. It was cloudless.

On my way home I checked my answering machine on the car phone.

You have one new message.

"Sunny, it's Tony Gault. I'm in town, at the Four Seasons, and I have a large rolling donut I don't know what to do with. Suggestions?"

I listened to the message again and smiled. He certainly wasn't reliable. But he had been fun. Time to branch out. Time to give in to impulse. Time to give Tony a second chance. And if it turned out not to be time . . . nothing wrong with fun.

ISIS publish a wide range of books in large print, from fiction to biography. Any suggestions for books you would like to see in large print or audio are always welcome. Please send to the Editorial department at:

ISIS Publishing Ltd.
7 Centremead
Osney Mead
Oxford OX2 0ES
(01865) 250 333

A full list of titles is available free of charge from:
Ulverscroft large print books

(UK)
The Green
Bradgate Road, Anstey
Leicester LE7 7FU
Tel: (0116) 236 4325

(Australia)
P.O Box 953
Crows Nest
NSW 1585
Tel: (02) 9436 2622

(USA)
1881 Ridge Road
P.O Box 1230, West Seneca,
N.Y. 14224-1230
Tel: (716) 674 4270

(Canada)
P.O Box 80038
Burlington
Ontario L7L 6B1
Tel: (905) 637 8734

(New Zealand)
P.O Box 456
Feilding
Tel: (06) 323 6828

Details of **ISIS** complete and unabridged audio books are also available from these offices. Alternatively, contact your local library for details of their collection of **ISIS** large print and unabridged audio books.